u n d e r c u r r e n t

y
b

NEWEST
PRESS

Library and Archives Canada Cataloguing in Publication
Metikosh, Anne, 1954-
Undercurrent / Anne Metikosh.

ISBN 1-896300-87-1

I. Title.

PS8576.E84U64 2005   C813'.6   C2004-906668-4

Cover and interior design: Ruth Linka
Cover image: Gordon Lewis
Author photo: Kate Metikosh

 Canada Council   Conseil des Arts
for the Arts   du Canada

 Canadian   Patrimoine
Heritage   canadien

NeWest Press acknowledges the support of the Canada Council for the Arts
and the Alberta Foundation for the Arts, and the Edmonton Arts Council
for our publishing program. We also acknowledge the financial support of
the Government of Canada through the Book Publishing Industry
Development Program (BPIDP) for our publishing activities.

NeWest Press
201–8540–109 Street
Edmonton, Alberta T6G 1E6
(780) 432-9427
www.newestpress.com

1   2   3   4   5   08   07   06   05

PRINTED AND BOUND IN CANADA

For Serge,
who gave me the idea

CHAPTER **ONE**

The day started like any other Monday.

My alarm clock shrilled no sinister warning. There was no mysterious message in my mailbox, no furtive glance from an enigmatic stranger on the street. Nothing but the usual pangs of morning-after guilt because, once again, I had squandered my Sunday night sleep for a book.

At seven-thirty I stumbled, bleary-eyed, into the office, scalded my tongue on overbrewed coffee, and swore as I spilled it setting the cup down. Our office manager, Joan, primmed her lips at me.

"Good morning, Charlotte."

Only Joan and my mother insist on calling me that; everybody else is fine with Charlie. Charlotte reminds me of swooning Victorian maidens, though I suppose it was inevitable when you take into account an older sister named Jane and a succession of semi-aristocratic hounds all called Rochester. Come to think of it, Nicholas used to call me Charlotte too, but I try not to dwell on that.

On my desk, my in-basket loomed like Mount St. Helens, ready to blow. I glanced at the picture tacked to the wall next to it. My six-year-old niece, Emily, had immortalized me standing in the woods surrounded by wild animals of dubious origin, a fatuous grin on my face. I looked like a cross between Grizzly Adams and a Girl Scout. One of the office clowns had added the witty caption, "Portrait of a conservation officer gone mad." I sighed and sat down to work.

Half a day's paper shuffling is all I can tolerate, which is one of the reasons I became a CO in the first place. It's also a job that combines my love of the wilderness with the lure of indoor plumbing. I spent a dutiful morning wading through a Sisyphean mound of paper before heading out to the field primed by a QuickieBurger. By one fifteen I was tooling along Range Road northwest of the town proper.

Geddes Lake sits firmly anchored in Precambrian shield like a six-legged spider in a rocky web. Its body is a motley collection of the same businesses, shops, and restaurants found in any other town, anywhere in the country. Its legs are what give it character. The longest extends eastward past the hospital to the goldmine that employs about a third of the local population. The stubbiest is sheathed in government offices whose steel and glass facades mirror the vast hinterland they administer. The third leg is bent, and where it crooks like a knee, it holds the diminutive university that serves the scattered population of the region. The other three are referred to collectively as the burbs. Geddes Lake boasts a population of ten thousand more or less permanent residents. Their homes reflect the people themselves; so many unique finishes and colours have been used in their building that 'patchwork quilt' best describes the overall look.

I was driving with my eye on the passing scenery and my mind on a report I was writing.

A local contractor had been busy clearing a site near the Posquatch River, levelling it to the specifications of a builder with grandiose ideas for the monied outdoorsmen who swell our ranks in season, and little conscience about the destruction of natural habitat. He had already wiped out some prime spawning grounds and was well on his way to narrowing part of the river to a channel when we slapped him with an injunction. I was mentally framing the conclusion to my report when a bull moose erupted from the woods to my right and halted abruptly in the middle of the road.

I hit the brakes hard. My car fishtailed and skidded in the dirt, leaving me slewed sideways, a broad target for any oncoming traffic. Luckily there was none.

The moose was supremely indifferent to me. I, on the other hand, was only too aware of the potential damage his half-ton bulk could inflict and graciously yielded him the right of way. Bullwinkle stood in the road, head back, nose up, testing the air. Searching, no doubt, for a sign of cows in heat. The last ribbons of velvet still hung bloodily from his antlers, but the tines would be stripped bare in time for the bull's first sparring matches over breeding rights. I never tired of these chance encounters.

Of all the memberships we use to identify ourselves— race, creed, sex, occupation—the one that is most forgotten, and yet holds the greatest potential for healing, is place. This is my place. Here in the woods and lakes of my beat are stored the most treasured memories of my life, my cache of conviction and contentment, waiting for me to draw on whenever I feel the need. This place and its creatures are the cornerstones of my life, though it's infinitely more satisfying to watch a moose browsing contentedly in a swamp than blocking a roadway. No telling how long this one might be parked. I tooted my horn. The bull stared at me for a minute, then moved off, grotesquely muscular on stilt-like legs.

Once my train of thought is broken, I have a hard time getting back on track. I mentally abandoned my report and flipped on the radio. Talk show host Dave Fredericks was well into an interview with Frank Dennison, environmental activist and founder of Save Our Planet. He was asking whether Dennison objected to being characterized as an eco-terrorist. SOP's primary spokesman had a confrontational style that didn't allow for any point of view other than his own. He answered in his familiar boom-box voice, full of jovial good fellowship, like a TV game show host.

"Frankly Dave, anything that calls attention to our cause is fine by me. If people see us as environmental commandos, so much the better. We are, after all, warriors of a sort. Fighting the most important battle of all time." Dennison's voice rose passionately. "The Battle To Save Our Planet!"

The capitals were clearly audible.

"Existence," Dennison went on forcefully, "is the fundamental right of every creature on this planet. Homo sapiens has too often violated this right in its single-minded quest for its own advancement and the fulfilment of its self-indulgent desires."

Here we go, I thought, gritting my teeth as he embarked on a long, polysyllabic, and largely unintelligible monologue about the nature of the universe.

It's not that I disagreed with him in principle. Technology has advanced to the point where the monkeys are overrunning the jungle, zealously turning the mean-ingless into the priceless, while the truly priceless is reduced to dust. But slogans, stunts, and lawbreaking in the name of a higher moral purpose won't change that; they only grant the illusion of redress.

Impatiently, I jabbed the off button, picked up the phone, and got the message that sent me out to Finger Lake in search of Jim Griffith.

CHAPTER **TWO**

Joan answered on the second ring.

"Hi, it's Charlie. Any messages?"

"Just one, " Joan said. "Jim Griffith wants you to take a look at something out at his place."

"Oh? Did he say what?"

"Noo-o. He sounded a bit excited though."

That gave me pause. Excited was not a word I normally associated with Jim Griffith, who had the steady eye and measured speech of a deliberate thinker.

I glanced at my watch. It was three-thirty. I should have plenty of time to stop by the old man's cabin and maybe cadge a cup of coffee. I wanted to make it back to Geddes Lake before the hardware store closed at six. A slow leak in my bathroom faucet had kept me awake the night before, counting the seconds of silence between maddeningly regular drips. In desperation, I had finally stuffed a washcloth into it.

Five miles down the road, just over the misnamed Highrise Hill, I made a right turn by a weathered signpost whose neatly chiselled letters read James Griffith (Fisherman).

The rutted track to Jim's cabin wound through woods where seedlings struggled to reach a sky glimpsed only in patches through the tops of high trees, and wisps of grey moss, like the beards of old men, hung from dead branches. The track ended abruptly, in a quiet clearing of green shadow and broken sunbeams marked by the twisted, lightning-scarred trunk of a once great pine, now pathetically diminished.

My boots made no noise on the springy earth, but from under my feet a grouse suddenly startled up into the air with a cry and was gone before I had a chance to see it. I thought the sound might alert Jim to my presence, but I heard no welcoming hail. I went around to the porch overlooking the lake and called, "Anybody home?" through the screen door. No answer.

I turned to scan the waterfront.

Evidently, Jim had set out to do some fishing. Rod and tackle lay heaped on the dock, waiting to be loaded into his aluminium boat, Kingfisher, which now drifted, empty and aimless, ten feet from shore. Off to the right, parallel to the dock, jutted a large, rocky outcropping. Just beyond it lay a motionless sprawl of khaki and red plaid.

Oh dear God, I thought. No.

I scrambled down the hill to the lake, cursing and clumsy in my haste, though it was clear there was no need to hurry. Even from a distance there was no mistaking the curiously huddled shapelessness of death.

Jim Griffith lay half in, half out of the water. A slight gash marked his temple. It looked as though Kingfisher had broken free of its mooring and in wading out to grab it, the old man had lost his footing on the slick rocks, hitting his head as he fell. The injury did not look fatal in itself, but Jim had fallen face down into six inches of water.

He couldn't have been dead very long when I arrived for, although flies were busily swarming, there was no sign of larger predators. I was grateful for that small mercy. Dealing with death is unpleasant enough without scavengers to cope with as well.

Jim's string bean physique gave me hope he would not be too heavy for me to move. Grabbing him by the shoulders, I managed to drag him around and up out of the water, and dropped onto the pebbled shore beside him.

James Griffith, Fisherman.

Actually, he was a retired tax accountant with a life-long passion for fishing. The day he turned sixty-five, Jim had unplugged his computer, sold his apartment, and moved north from Toronto to the isolated cabin on Finger Lake. Since then, lounging behind the wheel of a bright red Blazer, he had made the twice-weekly trip to town for laundry and supplies. He kept a cell phone at the cabin for emergencies only, preferring to do his socializing over a beer at The Angler.

I had looked in on Jim regularly over the past five years. It's part of my job to keep tabs on residents living outside the town limits. Usually it's just a question of a quick look-see, checking to make sure that this one hasn't been taken ill and that one hasn't shot himself in the foot. They aren't really social visits: people who have chosen to live so far removed from mainstream society have done so for a reason. Jim was different. Though he enjoyed living alone in the solitary splendour of "his" lake, he was always pleased to see me, happy to debate with a fellow amateur the relative merits of the wet versus the dry fly. It tickled his sense of humour that a woman should be as keen on fishing as any man. Over the years my visits to his cabin had evolved into something of a ceremonial high tea, complete with coffee and biscuits, but until today Jim had never asked to see me. I wondered what had been on his mind.

I sat quietly beside him for a few minutes, seeing in memory a man full of life and a passion for living simply, the planes and angles of his face animated by a keen intelligence. Gone. Vanished in an instant, with the frightening finality that has sent people diving for religious cover since time began.

Tears help some over the worst of it, but they don't work for me. I haven't cried in years. I think I used up a lifetime supply during the private war that was my marriage to Nicholas. In that campaign, tears had quickly become useless props. They couldn't mend my broken heart, and it had taken a trip to emergency to fix my broken arm.

I looked at the quiet body beside me, forcing myself to acknowledge the finality of the stiffening limbs and unresponsive features. How quickly personality had deserted the frame, leaving only an empty shell, like a house abandoned by its owner.

With a sigh, I covered Jim's face with my jacket and went back up the hill to make the necessary calls.

CHAPTER **THREE**

The coroner ruled Jim Griffith's death accidental and confirmed my belief that drowning, not injury, was the cause. His body was released for burial; his executor would make the trip north to handle the details. News of the accident spread quickly along well-travelled lines, and the town's social machinery clicked into gear.

Geddes Lake was virgin bush country back in the days when its founder, Sir Henry Geddes, was just plain Harry, a prospector looking for gold. In 1908 he found it and staked the first of twelve prosperous claims along what was to become known as Geddes's Golden Mile. He spent a good few years developing the area's lucrative mineral resources, made himself a small fortune, married several pretty women (one at a time), and swept out of town with the gold dust still clinging to the soles of his shoes. In keeping with his newly acquired title, he built himself a mansion in Ottawa and tried, without success, for a Senate appointment. In the mid-thirties, rising taxes forced him out of the country, an excuse that still hasn't gone out of fashion. Harry found himself a warm island retreat and began, slowly and pleasurably, to drink himself to death.

Meanwhile, at Geddes Lake, timber was cut, roads and railways were built, and a thriving mining community had its heyday. These days, only the Limberlost mine is still producing. But regional government has moved in. So has the university. At certain times of the year, we are besieged by the kind of tourist who heads north to really get away from it all and the local outfitters and guides do a brisk business. The rest of the time things are quiet enough to turn a memorial service into a major social event. Jim would have been especially pleased at the turnout for his: he loved a good party. He had no close relatives, but fishing cronies and other locals mingled in the reception room at Smith's Funeral Home, munching on sandwiches provided gratis by The Angler and drinking gallons of coffee as fast as they were brewed.

Making my way through the crowd for my own refill, I bumped heavily into a woman I didn't recognize and whose stylish look announced she was no local. The well-cut black suit had certainly not been purchased at Faye's Dress Shoppe, nor had the sleek hairdo come from Cutz for the Family. She stood uncomfortably aloof, a city fish out of her depth in the backwater.

"Sorry," I apologized, motioning to the cup in her hand. "I hope I haven't done any damage."

"Not at all. It was empty."

"Would you like a refill? There's plenty. I'm Charlie Meikle, by the way."

She inclined her head rather formally. "Jim's guardian angel." Her tone was less than friendly but, though she obviously didn't want to, good breeding won out and she offered me her hand. "I'm Jim's lawyer. Laura Rhodes."

I raised an eyebrow. Jim had mentioned Laura fondly from time to time, but the picture he had shown me was of a fresh-faced girl. The rather severe woman in front of me looked to be in her early thirties, trim and well-groomed, with that exterior gloss that speaks of aerobics classes and careful diet. Instinctively, she and I had squared off, like duellists assessing the competition. I was about two inches taller and maybe fifteen pounds heavier, none of it fat. My figure was earned outdoors, not in, and fed by what my mother calls meat-and-pota-toes cooking. I thought my hair gave me an edge; hers looked like it required regular salon maintenance, mine, when it wasn't tucked into a French braid, hung thick and straight half way down my back and needed only an occasional trim. On the other hand, Laura had nicer jewellery and very classy shoes. I consoled myself that neither would be much use in the bush.

I smiled. "Jim mentioned you, too. I'm sorry. You knew each other a long time."

"Yes." The full stop did not invite further comment. As a conversationalist, I thought, Laura Rhodes certainly led the field. Garbo also ran. I shrugged and started to move away.

"Ms. Meikle."

"Charlie," I said automatically.

"Charlie," she acknowledged. Her smile was rueful. "I apologize. I'm being rude and rather childish."

She had me hooked. Childishness isn't a fault most adults admit to easily. It suggests all that jealousy and spite we're supposed to outgrow—not that anybody ever does, of course.

I gestured toward the coffee urn. We stood in line wait-ing to refill our cups.

"I've known Jim nearly all my life," Laura said. "He was my father's accountant and, over the years, their professional relationship became a personal one. Jim didn't have much family of his own, so he sort of attached himself to ours."

I watched Laura stirring milk into her coffee, enjoying the swirling patterns it made on the inky surface before it was absorbed.

"Have you ever been married?" she asked suddenly.

I gave a brief nod, which she interpreted correctly.

"I haven't. Maybe that's why I didn't understand what happened with my parents. They always seemed happy enough to me, but what do kids know? Anyway, they split up when I was fourteen. The only good part was I got to be a bridesmaid. Twice. I bounced around between them for a while, but they were busy, and I'd become sort of a part-time kid to them."

Laura told her story in the detached tone of an observer watching a play that scarcely holds her interest. Only when she mentioned Jim Griffith did any warmth come into that cool, professional voice.

"He was my touchstone," she said. "He steered me into law, and he became my first client. You know, when Jim moved up here, I thought he was crazy. I kept waiting for him to get bored and come back to the city. Then he started writing about you." She shook her head. "I felt like a kid, mad at the world because she wasn't daddy's princess any more."

I stared hard at the mug in my hand, unwilling to meet Laura's eye while I groped for an appropriate response. After Nicholas, I'd tried a few counselling sessions, hoping to be able to unburden myself and find some measure of comfort, but I discovered I couldn't open up to a stranger any better than I could to a friend. Eventually, I had decided I'd have to work out my own solutions. I wished other people would do the same.

I was rescued from embarrassment by the sudden materialization of the head honcho of Smith's Funeral Home, Mr. Smith himself: a thin grey man in a thin grey suit. He spoke in a hushed murmur appropriate to the occasion. It was hard to believe he was the resident stand-up comedian at The Angler on Saturday nights.

"Excuse me, Charlie, but I need to speak to Ms. Rhodes for a moment." Turning to her, he lowered his sepulchral tone still further. "The urn is ready, ma'am. If you would care to step into my office?"

Laura hesitated. It's hard facing loss alone; grief is so often tempered with guilt.

"Would you like me to come along?"

She shot me a grateful look and I pointed her in the direction of the hall. A quick right brought us into Mr. Smith's inner sanctum, appropriately, if unimaginatively, decorated in sombre maroon and grey. Like recalcitrant schoolgirls facing the principal, we sat stiffly upright on hard-backed chairs, while Mr. Smith solemnly pronounced the necessary strictures regarding disposition of the remains. He coughed delicately into his fist.

"Should you not wish to purchase an interment site, a certain amount of, ah, discretion is advised in the disposal of the ashes. Public health codes, you know." He made a small gesture that both denied responsibility for government statutes and disclaimed liability for any possible transgressions. Ten minutes later, formalities observed, Mr. Smith accepted Laura's cheque and politely held the door.

"So, what happens now?" I asked. "Back to Toronto?"

"Not yet." Laura caught her lower lip between her teeth. "Jim wanted his ashes scattered at the lake. Unfortunately, I never quite managed to get up here to visit, so I don't know exactly where his cabin is." She hesitated, and I could tell it cost her something to ask, "I don't suppose you . . . ?"

"Sure," I said, trying to mean it. "No problem."

CHAPTER **FOUR**

The glade was half shadowed when we arrived, the sun slanting through the trees at an angle lower than when I had last been there. Jim's cabin looked forlorn and strangely vulnerable in the yellow grey light. I set the urn containing his ashes on the desk.

We had stopped by her motel long enough for Laura to change into silk shirt, designer jeans, and polished loafers, and I considered the shortcomings of my own wardrobe while I traded funeral wear for the khakis and pullover I always keep in my car. Encounters with mud and blood are pretty common in my line of work; I like to have clean clothes on hand when I need them.

We wandered down to the water, where I dutifully pointed out the spot where I had found Jim's body. Laura gazed at it in silence for a long moment. Then she moved gingerly out along the dock, picking her way to the far end where she settled slowly, like a cat. I watched, half expecting her to brush off the wood first so as not to dirty her jeans. She seemed to be all right, so after a minute I left her there, alone with her memories, and her regrets, and went back up to the cabin.

I looked at the urn. Beside it lay the cell phone Jim had used to call me on Monday, and again I wondered what had been on his mind. Maybe something to do with the poachers who had lately become a serious problem? Black bears are the favoured target around Geddes Lake.

Jim had taken a strong stand on the issue, and he had been in the process of establishing PoachWatch, a group designed to operate like a good neighbour program, with everyone keeping an eye on everyone else. Feeling about it ran high in town, some for, some against what Jim was trying to do. There'd been some nasty comments and a few veiled threats, but nothing serious.

I glanced around. Propped up against a corner cupboard were the posters Jim had planned to distribute. While we had discussed them in detail the week before, this was the first time I'd seen the finished product. Superimposed in black over a verdant forest was a line drawing of a hunter shooting out a message in bullets: Report a Poacher. Call 522-BEAR. The billboards were attractively laid out, but I wasn't sure Jim would have thought them worth a special trip out here.

One thing bothered me. Why, having called me, had Jim been getting ready to go fishing?

In my mind's eye I saw him, full of purpose, heading down to the shore laden with fishing gear. I watched him untying the Kingfisher; dropping the painter, reaching for the drifting boat, slipping, falling, drowning. I shook my head. Something didn't fit that picture.

The tackle had still been lying heaped on the dock when I arrived. Why would Jim—or anyone—untie his boat before loading his gear? Another vagrant thought nagged at my subconscious, but the harder I tried to make it surface, the farther away it shied.

"Charlie?"

Laura's voice startled me. I turned sharply, and a flash of orange hanging by the door caught my eye. It was Jim's lifejacket, the one he wore every single time he went fishing. "My second skin," he had called it. James Griffith, (Fisherman), had been unable to swim, and he had never ventured out on the lake without his lifejacket.

Something must have shown in my expression because Laura asked, "What is it?" with quick concern. I looked at her. Despite her efforts at concealment, her puffy eyelids gave her away. She had splashed lake water on her face, effectively erasing both tears and makeup; she looked defenceless, a woman wounded by loss. Any doubts about how Jim had died could wait, at least until he had been properly laid to rest. I shrugged off Laura's question.

"It's nothing. Are you okay?"

She nodded briefly, then gestured toward the urn. "Do you think we could go out on the lake now?"

"Sure. Would you rather go alone?"

"No, please, I'd like you to come. You knew Jim. You understood his attachment to this place." She paused. "He invited me up often. I never came. I was always too busy. Too damn busy." Tears threatened again, and she quickly turned to stare out the window. I gave her time, my mind drifting to unwelcome memories of my father and his death at the hands of a drunk driver. I had been sixteen at the time, full of teenage rebellion, spending too much of my energy in loud and acrimonious confrontation with him. On the day he died, my father and I had butted heads with particular acrimony and I had loudly wished him out of my life. In the years since, I had learned to forgive myself that childish outburst, but my regret at never having the chance to know him as a friend had never lessened, and there were still many days I missed him, and desperately wished him back so that I could tell him so. Death, I thought drearily, forces you to leave so many words unspoken.

"Let's go," I said, abruptly shaking off melancholy.

I had retrieved Jim's boat from the middle of the lake while the medical professionals dealt with his body, and Kingfisher, a fifteen-foot Lund with a little 10 horsepower outboard, was once again tethered to the dock. Even a small motor like that can make a disturbing amount of noise, so I turned instead to the canoe resting on its gunwales under the trees. It was an old cedar strip freighter that Jim had used for his more adventurous fishing trips beyond the confines of the lake, where portaging and camping would be required. I carried it to the water's edge, steadied it while Laura got hesitantly in, then stepped in myself, and pushed off.

We glided across the still water in silence broken only by the dip and splash of the paddle. Finger Lake was no more than half a mile wide. It didn't take long to reach the far side, where, in summer, water lilies bloomed.

"Here?" I suggested.

"Perfect." Laura opened the little canister and gently sprinkled its contents over the water. For a moment, Jim Griffith's ashes clung to the surface, as though reluctant to lose their hold on light and air. Then, like dust motes in a sunbeam, they drifted slowly down to rest on the lake bottom. Laura watched wordlessly, her eyes bright with tears.

I quoted softly. "I went to the woods because I wished to live deliberately, to front only the essential facts of life, and see if I could not learn what it had to teach, and not, when I came to die, discover that I had not lived."

The poet's words floated away into the dusky stillness that precedes the many voices of the night. The sun balanced at horizon's edge, burnishing the lake water to a rich copper gold. The silence was a balm to the spirit.

Eventually Laura stirred and sighed.

"Was that Whitman?" she asked.

"Thoreau."

We paddled back across the lake in a newly companionable silence. Here and there a fish rose to a fly, sending delicate ripples skimming across the black surface of the water. The crickets had started their noisy chirping and as we neared the dock, a couple of tree frogs cheerfully joined in. Once again, I steadied the canoe for Laura, then dragged it back up under the shelter of the trees. Invisible in the growing dark, a loon sent its crazy laugh echoing across the water.

We picked our way carefully back up the path to Jim's cabin. Inside, the electric light provided by the small generator seemed almost harsh. Laura shuffled half-heartedly through some of the papers on Jim's desk, then made a brief tour of inspection, mentally cataloguing the trappings of a lifestyle totally foreign to her. I watched with some amusement as she opened the large storage cupboard. Several pairs of rubber waders hung next to a fishing vest festooned with gadgets. Nets of varying shapes and sizes were neatly stacked on the shelf beside them. Place of honour was held by a beautifully carved wooden box. Laura lifted the lid. Inside were a dozen small plastic boxes, each filled with a gaudy assortment of flies, all hand tied. She shook her head in disbelief.

The cabin itself was plainly furnished, the only decoration being a handsomely mounted trout hung over the fireplace. Apart from the few he kept and ate, Jim had been a catch-and-release fisherman. This rainbow was the exception; he had done the taxidermy himself. Laura viewed it with distaste.

"How am I ever going to sort out all this stuff?" she said. "I don't even know what half of it is. And I certainly have no use for it."

Impulsively, I offered, "If you like, I could go through it, give some of the fishing gear to a few of Jim's friends, weed out the papers on his desk and send them down to you. Okay?"

She nodded enthusiastic agreement.

"What about furniture and so on?" I said.

"I'll likely sell it with the cabin. There's no room in my apartment and it . . ." she made a face, "well, it's not exactly my style."

"You'll definitely sell the place, then?"

"Oh, I think so. What else would I do with it? Perhaps you could put me in touch with a local realtor?"

"Sure. Whenever you're ready."

On the way back to town, I asked what plans she had for dinner.

"Pick up something at the motel restaurant I suppose. I'm not very hungry."

"You'd have to be starving to eat there. I've got some trout at my place, if you'd like."

She smiled. "Trout would be great."

CHAPTER **FIVE**

I puttered around the kitchen of my little house while Laura inspected my living room. She commented favourably, as everyone did, on the fieldstone fireplace. In front of it lounged a couch and chairs selected on the basis of comfort rather than style. The north wall of the house is completely covered by shelves I've built myself to accommodate an ever growing hoard of books. Friends have accused me of bordering on anal when it comes to collecting and cataloguing. I'm an inveterate pack rat who doesn't read Better Homes and Gardens. My decorating scheme is beige. Beige paint, beige carpet, beige furniture. The monotony is relieved by splashes of colour in the Inuit prints on the walls and the fire that perpetually gives life to the room. Soft lamplight, drinks tray close at hand—home.

"There's a CD player in the cabinet there," I called from the kitchen. "Disc's already in."

"Found it," Laura replied. A moment later the clear, uncluttered notes of a clarinet filled the room.

In the kitchen I tore off some lettuce leaves and put them in a bowl of ice water to crisp. On the counter a trout lay gutted, ready to be stuffed with the wild rice gently simmering on the stove. I took a bottle of white wine from the refrigerator and popped the cork. Laura appeared in the doorway.

"Great house," she said. "I had to go upstairs . . ."

"It's the only way to the bathroom," I agreed.

My house is very small: two bedrooms, one bath up; living room, kitchen, and study down. Knocking down the study wall had given me a large open living space with the fireplace at one end and a picture window framing the woods at the other. A galley kitchen runs the width of the house at the back. I had established the no man's land between living room and kitchen as a dining alcove.

Laura sniffed appreciatively. "Something smells good," she said, lifting the lid on the rice. "And by the way, did you know your faucet leaks up there?"

With all that had happened, I had forgotten to pick up a washer. I made a mental note to do it in the morning.

Laura accepted a glass of wine and stood watching from the doorway as I drained the lettuce, wrapped it, and put it in the fridge. I took the rice off the stove, used some of it to stuff the trout, and dumped the rest into a casserole dish. The fish I covered loosely with foil. As I popped it into the oven, I pointed Laura in the direction of linen and cutlery and told her to make herself useful while I measured oil and vinegar for the salad dressing.

"You're going to a lot of effort," Laura said. "My idea of cooking is thawing out something low-cal from Freezer Gourmet."

I laughed. "I like to cook. Actually, I like to eat. The cooking part is just a means to an end. Somehow it increases my pleasure in sitting down to a meal. Which we can do now."

We chatted idly as we ate, bridging the gap between city mouse and country mouse with the common ground of books and music.

"You're not at all what I expected," Laura confided.

We had finished dinner and retired to the living room. Three-year-old apple wood burned in the fireplace, fragrant and vaguely reminiscent of a summer's day.

"What did you expect, exactly?"

"Oh, I don't know. Some kind of overgrown Girl Scout I guess, all hairy knees and roughing it in the bush. Certainly not poetry and stuffed trout."

"Hairy knees?"

Laura shrugged.

I placed my right hand over my heart and said, "I solemnly affirm that my legs are as smooth as wax and a razor can make them." I dropped my hand. "And my mother spoon fed us poetry from the cradle."

"Us?"

"My sister Jane and me. Jane teaches poetry at Western. I spent a lot of time in my teens pretending to despise it, mostly because I couldn't understand it. I came back to it eventually, in a narrow kind of way. Mostly, I like poems that express the feelings I have about living here. The rest of it's too hard."

"Have you always lived in Geddes Lake?"

"No, we moved all over the place. My dad was a mining consultant. We'd been here about two years when he died. Jane was already away at university. My mother hung in 'til I was through high school, but she made tracks as soon as the first grandchild came along. She's at Jane's now as a sort of live-in nanny. I visit them a couple of times a year."

I deliberately omitted mention of marriage from my little recitation. After high school, I'd stayed on in Geddes

Lake, taking a general science degree at the university with some vague notion of following in my father's footsteps. A brief encounter in a local bar changed my mind, and I had panted down to Toronto in the wake of Nicholas Ratcliffe, a handsome, sexy, intelligent man who hid a vicious temper behind a smiling urbanity. Apart from a broken arm, people tell me I came out of our relationship relatively unscathed. The truth is, things always look a lot different on the outside from the way they feel on the inside. In the last six years, I may have achieved some measure of outer calm, but it's maintained only by constant inner diligence.

On the hearth a log fell apart, sending a shower of sparks flying upward.

Laura said quietly, "What was wrong, back there at Jim's cabin? And don't bother with denials, Charlie. I know when someone's holding out on me."

I rose and poked the fire back into shape, adding another log before I turned to face her. She looked steadily back at me, once more the composed and efficient lawyer.

"All right," I said slowly and I told her about the life-jacket still hanging on the back of Jim's door. To me, it was a damning indication that the scene at Finger Lake had been staged.

Laura didn't see it that way. "Mightn't he have simply planned to go back for it?" she asked.

I shook my head. "I don't think so, no. Jim put that life jacket on first thing whenever he was going down to the boat. He wouldn't bother making two trips."

"I suppose not," Laura said doubtfully. "But he was

there at the waterfront, wasn't he? And it was obvious he was going fishing; all his stuff was on the dock."

"On the dock, yes. Not in the boat."

"So what?"

"Well, when you're going fishing, you load your boat first, then cast it off. There's no point making things awkward for yourself by doing it the other way around. That's number one. Number two, we know that in Jim's case, going fishing always meant wearing a life jacket. So, if he planned to go out, why was the life jacket still hanging on its peg in the cabin?"

Laura shook her head.

"There's another thing," I pointed out. "The day he died, Jim called my office and asked me to come see him. Apparently he had something to show me. In the five years that I've known him, Jim has never once called me. He knew when I'd drop by. Why not just wait? What was so urgent on that day of all days?"

"That's coincidence."

"I don't believe in coincidence."

"What, then?"

"Cause and effect."

Laura was silent, chewing her lower lip in a habit of concentration I already recognized, staring into the fire with the same brooding expression I had seen at the lake. Long minutes ticked by.

Finally she spoke. "All right then, given all that, what are you suggesting?"

I shrugged, palms up.

"I don't really know," I admitted. "But oddities stand out. They give rise to questions. I don't know the answers."

CHAPTER **SIX**

Sunday dawned in a cold, grey drizzle: the kind of day to cozy up in a chair with a good book. It took firm resolve to turn my back on the fireplace and a Tony Hillerman novel to head out to Finger Lake. Laura had flown back to Toronto, leaving me in possession of the keys to the cabin and her authorization to examine Jim's belongings. She still wasn't convinced that my questions had much merit, but we'd both loved Jim and she was willing to let me poke around on that basis. Armed with a thermos of coffee and some fresh bagels (Geddes Lake has the best bagel shop west of Montreal), I set off for Finger Lake, hoping to locate whatever it was that Jim had wanted to show me. I thought finding it would go a long way toward proving—or disproving—my growing suspicion that Jim's accident had been arranged: that he had been murdered.

The cabin was cold, uninviting. Without knowing exactly what I was looking for, I started my search in the living room and worked my way methodically through the papers on Jim's desk, keeping an eye open for anything that looked out of place or recently disturbed. I did not expect whatever it was to be hidden. Jim had phoned requesting that I come to see it. He would have kept it close at hand and it should be there still—unless someone had removed it. Why anyone might have done that, I had no idea.

I found no evidence of an earlier search: no gaps in the pigeonholes, no indication that anything was missing. What I did find was a series of neatly docketed invoices, all paid, catalogues of fishing equipment, tips on fly tying, letters from Laura. These last I put aside to send to her. There were several business cards tucked into the corner of the blotter. "Al's Small Engine Repairs," "Waterson's" (For all Your Outdoor Needs), "Burns Bait & Tackle."

I shuffled quickly through some miscellaneous stuff, stopping in surprise at a newspaper clipping of a protest rally organized by Save Our Planet, and illustrated by a photo of Frank Dennison in full cry. It was an unusual keepsake for a man like Jim. As far as I knew, he'd never supported the Save Our Planet publicity line. I shrugged. Maybe someone had sent it to him when they heard about his anti-poaching efforts.

Idly, I turned the pages of a leather-bound book marked Fishing Log. Jim's fine script filled the tidy columns, recording his catch by species, size, weight, where caught, and bait used. The entries, begun five years ago, ended the day before his death. Scribbled in the margin of the last page was the cryptic message, "Talk to Charlie!"

Outside, the drizzle had turned into a downpour. There was no heat on in the cabin and the chill air tickled my neck and wrists, left exposed by my sweater. I opened the thermos, letting the comforting aroma of hot coffee fill the room, and warmed my hands around the mug. Huddled in the overstuffed chair by the window, I studied Jim's log more closely. Talk to me about what? There was nothing remarkable about the fish Jim had caught. If anything, they were small. Unusually small? My interest quickened. I flipped back a few pages, comparing this year's catch with previous years'. A definite pattern began to emerge.

The fish population of a healthy lake is normally diverse. Many species of all ages are more or less equally represented. Given that his special interest was trout, that was reflected accurately enough in Jim's log. But over the last two years there had been a steady decline in the number of adult fish being caught. This year there was only one of any size. It was the final entry in the log, flagged by the notation to talk to me. I frowned. The evidence in the log suggested that something was interfering with the health of the aquatic community in Finger Lake. But what? Finger Lake was spring fed; there were no connecting waterways to affect it. It was not an outlet for any kind of industrial waste. So where was the problem coming from? I thought about it for a while without coming up with any answers.

My stomach growled. I was startled to note that it was well past lunchtime. Laying Jim's log aside, I toted my bagels into the kitchen in search of a knife. It occurred to me then that no one had yet cleaned out Jim's fridge. Suppressing a shudder at what I might find lurking within, I opened the door, only to find that in this, as in everything else, Jim had been a master of organization. The milk had gone skunky, but the other foodstuffs were tightly wrapped or frig-o-sealed and there were no green fuzzies growing anywhere. I packed the groceries into a box to take home with me. In the interest of thoroughness, I opened the freezer and there found the answer I had been looking for.

A full sized trout stared out at me: Jim's last catch. Through the plastic wrap that shrouded it, I could see that something was wrong with the fish's mouth. I peered at it more closely. No doubt about it, a tumour sprouted from its upper lip, giving it a lopsided look. Finally the penny dropped. Coupled with the information in the log, the trout made a damning statement about the quality of the water in Finger Lake.

But it went nowhere towards explaining what had happened to Jim Griffith.

CHAPTER **SEVEN**

By four o'clock I had searched through everything that seemed worth searching without turning up any clues to Jim's attacker. Some detective I'd turned out to be. I decided to call it a day, and lugged the box of groceries out to my car along with Jim's fishing log and the still frozen trout. Those two I could deal with in my official capacity. Unofficially, I felt a deep sense of frustration. Reviewing the facts as I knew them, I was still convinced that Jim Griffith's death had been more than a simple accident. All I needed was some evidence.

There was nothing to be found either in the cabin or on the waterfront: no signs of a struggle, no notes to mysterious strangers, only my own intuition that things were not as they appeared to be. It was time to take a different tack, if only I could decide what that tack was.

Meanwhile, duty called. There had been a new incidence of bear poaching to investigate; the report still had to be finished and added to our growing file. On Friday, a couple of hikers had come across yet another black bear carcass in a gully about five miles east of Finger Lake. That made the fourth one in two weeks shot down and gutted, carcass left to rot.

In Ontario, it's a chargeable offence to allow edible game to go to waste—and it's illegal to buy, sell, or barter body parts. But it's a tough crime to prosecute. Even when criminals are caught red-handed, sentences are often lenient and probation requirements difficult to enforce.

Licensed hunters have an annual quota of one bear each. Poachers are another matter. It's common knowledge that there is a brisk and lucrative trade these days in shipping black bear gallbladders to the Asian market. Taken a little at a time with liquor, galls are believed to cure a whole range of physical ailments, from backache to blood poisoning, not to mention their use as aphrodisiacs. I remember reading a year or so ago about some South Korean businessmen who made the national news after they imported thirty-five frozen black bears. They were selling the galls for up to twenty thousand dollars each.

Sometimes poachers sell the claws, head, and teeth too—like parts of a stripped-down car. In Asia, bear meat and bear paw soup are considered special occasion foods and they're becoming increasingly popular in some North American cities. In Geddes Lake, anything served au gratin is considered exotic.

The poachers we were looking for were not particular; the bears were being hacked to bits. The lure of easy money was proving irresistible to someone, which, given the prevailing economic climate, was hardly surprising.

The hikers had called in their find from the Donut Delight at the edge of town. I met them there and we drove out in convoy to take a look.

The bear had been dead about four days. Inexpert butchering and natural decay had turned it into a grisly mess. The hikers, a couple barely out of their teens, gave their statements in wavering tones. According to the boy, they had been in the area the week before and had passed three hunters, men, up on the ridge road. Spotting hunters during hunting season is hardly unusual, but they had remarked on these three because of their camouflage suits. Hunters tend to wear bright clothing so they can be easily spotted by other hunters and not mistaken for targets. The boy thought the tallest of the men had a dark moustache. The girl nodded agreement. She hadn't said much; she seemed to be busy trying to control a case of the queasies. I couldn't blame her. They were both relieved when I thanked them for their help and sent them on their way.

I got the camera out of the glove box and took photographs as quickly as I could, swearing quietly all the while and trying not to breathe too deeply. There were no cigarette butts or footprints to identify the bad guys, but bloodstains made it easy to trace the route they must have taken back up to the road and, presumably, a waiting vehicle.

I spent Sunday evening writing up my report on the incident.

First thing Monday morning I called Dr. Paul Ewing, a research biologist whose brain I had picked more than once over the years. I was a lowly first year student when we met at the University of Northern Ontario. He was a PhD candidate earning some extra cash working as lab assistant to the head of the department. While he produced a brilliant thesis on the spawning behaviour of lake trout, I scraped through with a bachelor's degree. He was engaged to Carole MacDonald when I met him. In the days when beer was all we could afford, the three of us produced the first comprehensive, exhaustively researched, and thoroughly documented treatise on brew establishments, greater and lesser, in the north.

When I was in my third year at the University, Paul, now Dr. Ewing, signed on with the Ministry of Natural Resources. After the disaster with Nicholas, he persuaded me to the same course. We still tour the pubs together, though not as often.

Paul answered my call on the third ring.

"Charlie Meikle," I said, "known in environmental investigative circles as Madame Sleuth."

"Come off it, it's too early in the morning for that, Charlie. My sense of humour doesn't kick in 'til noon."

It's good to know Mondays affect everyone the same way.

Officiously I said, "I have recently acquired some information regarding an aquatic enigma in your juris-diction."

"'Aquatic enigma'? Gimme a break. You're starting to sound like a policy paper."

"Just because you live in the seclusion of a research lab is no reason to put me down, Doc. You want to see what I've got, or not?"

"Come on over," he said and hung up. He didn't sound excited.

His eyes didn't exactly light up when I handed him what I'd found at the cabin either, but his mind engaged with an almost audible click as he went over the entries in Jim Griffith's log. I helped myself to some coffee. According to the Cosmo quiz, "How well do you handle stress?" which I read while waiting for the dentist to drill a hole in my mouth, I should really be cutting down on caffeine. Maybe, I thought, if I added milk and sugar, the coffee would taste so lousy I wouldn't want to drink it any more. I filled a mug to brimming and took a large mouthful of the unsweetened black brew.

Paul had started a tuneless humming as he jotted down some figures on a piece of foolscap. His foot tapped and he was nodding his head in time to some inaudible beat. I loved to watch him work, but after a few minutes he said irritably, "Haven't you got anyplace else to go? Some poor slob to ticket for fishing without a licence? I have to do a little research here and some lab work on the trout. I'll call you."

I went back to my own office and shuffled a few papers. I checked over some notes and the slides I had assembled for a presentation to the Grade ten class at the high school. Their teachers are big on promoting the three Rs—reduce, reuse, recycle. I try to focus on the broader picture: the relatedness of one ecosystem to another and how you can't mess up just one. I like to point out that humans are the only living things that are not necessary to the environment in which they live. It's a humbling thought.

I knocked off for the day around five thirty and headed over to The Angler. It's what some people might call a seedy bar, but what it lacks in decor it more than makes up for in ambience and draft beer. A lot of the Ministry people drop in there for a quick one on the way home. Thursday is payday; Mondays are pretty quiet.

Only a couple of tables were occupied when I went in. Half a dozen mine workers off the afternoon shift were getting down to serious business in the far corner. Rumour had it the Limberlost Mine was in a financial pickle that was about to be solved by an American takeover. That would mean layoffs and more local unemployment. Nobody liked the idea, but there wasn't much anybody could do about it. There weren't many Canadian companies with pockets deep enough to effect a rescue; if the mine shut down completely, so could Geddes Lake.

At the opposite end of the room two older men were having an animated discussion. I knew them both well enough to share a table, so I picked up my draft and sauntered over.

"How do, Charlie?" one of them barked. Les Mills, a scrawny little man with a voice like an old crow and manners to match, was the best fly fisherman in the region. He'd won the Golden Rod award three years runnning.

"Not bad, Les. You?" He gave me a thumbs up. I turned to the other man, a big guy with a forceful air and a serious expression. "And how are you, Mr. Purvis?"

Geoffrey Purvis had been principal of the high school when I was a kid and I still wasn't old enough to call him anything but Mr. Purvis. Somehow I don't think I ever will be.

"Well, thank you, Charlie," he said, pulling out a chair. "Have a seat. What's new at the Ministry? Have you turned up anything on the poacher problem yet?" I could feel myself beginning to squirm under the well-remembered Purvis stare. Its message was clear. I was not working up to my full potential; the problem could be solved; I had only to apply myself. I applied myself to my beer.

"What's the big deal, eh?" cawed Les. "If the govermint didn't spend all its time taxin' the hell out of the ordinary joe in the street, nobody'd need to poach the damn bears. Every time you turn around the govermint's takin' more money outta your pocket. GSTs and PSTs. Shit. The govermint oughta do somethin' about that for a change, 'stead a pickin' on some poor bugger who's just tryin' to get by." He looked at me accusingly. I looked right back.

"Got a particular poor bugger in mind, Les, or are you just making a general observation?" I asked.

Les dropped his belligerent gaze and studied his beer intently for a few moments before mumbling, "It's just an opinion, eh? A man's entitled to his opinion."

"No question."

"Doesn't mean he knows anythin' about anything."

"I couldn't agree more."

I heard a strange muffled sound coming from Mr. Purvis. There was no expression on his face, but he seemed to be having some kind of problem with his throat. He cleared it with a cough.

"I gotta go," Les said abruptly, pushing back his chair. "Gotta pick up a few things for the wife on my way home. You comin', Geoff?"

"No, I think I'll finish off my beer. I'll see you Thursday, Les."

"Right, then." He didn't say goodbye to me.

Mr. Purvis drained his glass. "Will you be attending the meeting on Thursday, Charlie?" I nodded. Every third Thursday evening, members of the Geddes Lake Rod and Gun Club meet over at the Legion. The club members are mostly men, of course, but there is a scattering of women, which is more than there used to be. The hunters discuss stalking techniques; the fishermen come bearing little bags of feathers and bits of fur and spend a couple of hours teaching each other to tie flies. Everybody airs his pet theory about the right time of day, the right kind of weather, the right rod to assure success. I once talked with an Ojibwa trapper who told me that none of that stuff is very important; getting what you're after has more to do with reading the water and knowing the feeding habits of the fish. Fish might not be very smart, but their survival instincts are finely tuned and there is great satisfaction in trying to convince one that a bit of fluff and a hook is food. I'm not very skilled at fly-casting myself. I'm better with a bait rod. I attend the club meetings because I enjoy the company. It's also a good way of picking up the current scuttlebutt.

"You seem to have had an unsettling effect on Les Mills, Charlie," said Mr. Purvis neutrally. "He left without finishing his beer."

"I noticed that. Do you think it was something I said?"

"Actually," Mr. Purvis replied, "I think it was something he said."

I nodded. "That was my impression, too."

Mr. Purvis smiled. I knew that smile. It meant that one of his dimmer pupils had finally shown some promise.

CHAPTER **EIGHT**

Paul Ewing called me Wednesday morning just as I was settling into my third cup of coffee.

"I've got some information on your 'aquatic enigma.' What's it worth to you?"

I thought about it for a minute. "Lunch at Dot's?"

He snorted. "I'm working for peanuts these days. See you there. Twelve fifteen."

Dot's is an institution in Geddes Lake. Dot herself opened the place in 1956 in what was then the middle of downtown. The centre of affairs has shifted slightly since then, but Dot's hasn't and Dot is still running it. Not much has changed in almost forty years. Dot's is an authentic old time diner with linoleum on the floor, swivel stools at the counter, and red vinyl seats in the booths that line one wall. Each table has its own miniature jukebox whose record selections have not been updated in twenty years. My personal favourite is "A Sixpack to Go." They don't write them like that any more.

I was searching my pockets for a quarter when Paul slid into the booth across from me. A waitress was with us thirty seconds later, smiling brightly, anxious to please. Women always hover over Paul like moths around a lightbulb. I adore him myself, but we've been friends for too long for it ever to be anything else. He never flirts, and the wedding band he acquired twelve years ago is always in plain view, but still, we all love him.

Both of us ordered clubhouse sandwiches and beer.

"Coors Light?" Paul scoffed when I stated my preference. "Isn't that kind of redundant? Better give me a Blue," he smiled at the waitress. She hustled off to fetch it with a sparkling smile. I had to assume she would get mine too.

The waitress, whose name was Kerri, with a happy face dotting the *i*, brought the beer in large chilled mugs and, ten minutes later, two toasted clubs stuffed with BLT and real meat, not turkey roll. The final item on the tray was a huge basket of home cooked fries. It's small wonder Dot has been in business so long.

Part way through the feast I popped the big question. "What have you got?"

Paul washed down a bite of sandwich with a mouthful of beer. "Some fact, some theory. All of it relevant to what you found. I won't waste your time with the usual caveats about sampling techniques and statistical analyses. Obviously, these are preliminary findings."

I nodded.

He went on, "Okay. As you know, a lot of toxic chemicals can't be detected in water because they exist at concentrations below the minimum detection levels of standard analytical procedures." I nodded again. I did know that. Paul went on, "So we tend to use fish as a sort of yardstick of water quality. Fish are terrific indicators of ecosystem health—or the lack of it—because they are not only exposed to aquatic contaminants, they bioaccumulate many of them. And lake trout are especially useful indicators of contamination for several reasons." He ticked them off on his fingers. "They're high on the food chain, which means they get bigger chemical doses than species lower down the chain, they have a high concentration of body fat for storing chemicals, they are extremely mobile, and they have a long life span, which means their exposure time is longer than other species. Are you with me so far?"

"I think so. But in my understanding, fish don't store toxic chemicals in their body fat; they metabolize them. Is that right?"

"Absolutely. And in the process, their systems are exposed to an almost endless combination of chemicals that somehow alter their normal biochemical and physiological functions. Sometimes the alterations manifest themselves as physical deformities."

"Like the tumour on that trout I brought you."

"Exactly," Paul nodded. "That much is fact. Now here's where the theory comes in. Toxic effects can occur at various levels of organization: from molecular and cellular changes in an individual—again, like what you found—right on up to changes in the population of a species and the diversity and abundance of species in a community. Take a hypothetical aquatic ecosystem stocked with trout, one like Finger Lake. A contaminant in that lake that alters, say, the production of sex hormones, will affect the structure of the fish's reproductive organs and the quality, quantity, and timing of eggs and sperm. That kind of severe disruption could cause reproductive failure, so, ultimately, the population of trout decreases and, as it does, the population of other species increases."

I frowned. "So you end up with a lot of carp or

alewife or something where there used to be trout."

"Right. Then you not only have a lot of fish nobody wants to eat, but you also have a lot of changes in the benthic, zooplankton, and phytoplankton populations."

"In effect, changing the lake's ecological structure."

"Who said you weren't educable?"

Paul signalled the waitress for a refill. I fiddled with the jukebox.

"So where does all this get us? The trout population in Finger Lake is obviously declining. According to the records Jim Griffith kept, hardly any of the existing population is surviving to adulthood. The few that do are deformed. Can you figure out what's causing it?"

Paul shrugged. "You're the sleuth, Charlie. I can tell you what's happening; it's up to you to figure out how. Just keep in mind that you don't have to dump chemicals directly into a lake to contaminate it. If they're leaching through the aquifer and getting into the groundwater, they could be coming from anywhere."

I thought about it on the way back to the office. How could chemical contaminants possibly be finding their way into Finger Lake? Any of the Great Lakes, sure; they are prime dumping grounds for all kinds of industrial waste. And, apart from the obvious effects of mining and logging, it's true that a lot of northern lakes have been stressed to their limits by the expansion of the towns and cottage communities that have grown up around them. But an isolated lake like Finger?

It could be coming from anywhere, Paul had said. Terrific, that gave me a nice wide field to play in. In the interests of narrowing it down a little, I decided to pick up some topographical maps when I went back to the office. There was virtually no heavy industry left in Geddes Lake. Only the Limberlost Mine was still producing and it was a good ten miles from Finger Lake. I figured the source of the contaminant had to be closer than that. Otherwise, its effects would have shown up in the less isolated lakes and streams in between, waterways that saw a lot more use than Finger Lake did. The top maps might give me a clue to other possibilities.

After my lunch meeting with Paul Ewing, the afternoon disappeared in a morass of phone calls and complaints. Someone had discovered a deer lying dead in a far corner of his property. The animal seemed to have died of natural causes, but the property owner wanted the carcass removed before unwelcome predators arrived.

Someone else had left a back door open too long and a skunk had wandered in and was now barricaded in a closet. Could we offer any advice on how to get rid of it— without offending it?

The phone rang again. An elderly lady named Irene Creighton demanded to know when I was going to put a stop to the traffic on the old Windrush Mine road late at night. "I've lived out here for forty-odd years, young lady, and I'm used to a lot of comings and goings, but to have to put up with that kind of disturbance in the middle of the night is too much! All that clanking around would be bad enough, but the language those men were using was absolutely disgraceful!"

I stifled a laugh and managed "I'm sorry to hear that, ma'am," politely enough. "It sounds to me as though someone had a midnight flat and didn't deal with it too gracefully. I'm afraid we have no jurisdiction over things like that." Mrs. Creighton hung up, still miffed.

By six o'clock it was getting dark and I was getting hungry, so I gathered up the maps I had collected from downstairs and headed home. My neighbour's son, Will, had already delivered my newspaper. As usual, it lay a good eight feet shy of the front door and I tripped over it on my way up the walk. Cursing, I retrieved it.

My halfhearted "tch" turned into a wholly disgusted "for crying out loud" when I saw the lead story. Frank Dennison's troop of eco-activists was pulling out all the stops in its latest bid for attention. Dressed in skeleton costumes and gas masks, they had dumped a dozen truck-loads of reeking garbage in front of Toronto's City Hall minutes before the arrival of local politicians and busi-nessmen who were meeting to discuss the proposed expansion of landfill sites in and around the city. The front page photo showed a bunch of fist-waving groupies being carted off to jail. On the ground a trampled placard read, "Keep our cities clean. Keep our cities green." In a call to Dennison's office, one enterprising journalist had secured the quote, "Politicos and big business yahoos cannot be allowed to pursue their current reckless waste disposal policies. Alternate methods must be found for dealing with the city's garbage and safe storage facilities located for the disposal of toxic waste."

That's great, Frank. There's a lot of original thinking behind that statement. What a great solution, too. Paying your flunkies to dump a load of trash in front of City Hall and spend a night in jail will certainly go a long way toward solving the problem. Crumpling up the paper, I used it to start the fire.

I made a quick tour of the kitchen and came up with some spaghetti and a salad. I eat salad most days in an ingrained revolt against cooked vegetables. I either eat them fresh or not at all.

After dinner I spread the top maps out on the table. Using Finger Lake as the midpoint, I worked my way around it in an expanding radius, noting contours, rock formations, and stream flows. When I got to the half mile circle, I struck gold, literally, in the shape of the Windrush Mine. As far as I knew, the mine had not been operating in the past ten years, but when I kept on going out to a five mile circumference and found nothing else remotely promising, I returned to it with a speculative eye. I had never heard of a case of mine effluents affecting the environment so many years after the fact, but I was no expert in hydrogeology and, I supposed, anything is possible. Before stirring up any hue and cry though, I thought I should take a trip out to the Windrush and have a look around myself.

My back creaked as I straightened up. I stretched, rolled up the maps, poured myself a brandy, and settled in front of the fire with the Hillerman novel I had so piously ignored on the weekend. Joe Leaphorn and Jim Chee were once again battling the bad guys and winning. I wish I had their tracking ability.

CHAPTER **NINE**

I missed the beginning of the Rod and Gun Club meeting. I must have picked up a nail on the way home from work on Thursday because, between my arrival home and setting out again two hours later, my right rear tire went flat. It was no big deal; I had a spare, but the inconvenience of messing around in the dark with jacks and tire irons put me in a foul mood. I've never been very philosophical over life's minor trials. When I was ten, I had one of those statement posters on my closet door that said, "It's not the mountain ahead that gets you down, it's the grain of sand in your shoe." Not much has changed since then. I threw the damaged tire into the back of my wagon. I would drop it off at Ray's Garage in the morning.

The minutes of the last meeting had been approved and the monthly financial statement presented by the time I arrived at the Legion Hall. As usual, the place was packed. Generally, the first hour of the meeting is devoted to club business, followed by a guest speaker who expounds on the topic of his choice for a while. Sometimes there is a slide presentation. By eight thirty we get down to the real business of the evening. Beer and conversation start to flow in roughly equal proportions as the club members pursue their individual lines of inquiry and interest. Hunters and trappers tend to migrate to one end of the room, anglers and fly fishermen to the other.

When I walked in, half a dozen people clustered

around the bar called out "How's it going, Charlie?"

I joined them long enough to say hello and buy myself a beer, then began to circulate. That night the prevailing topic of discussion was the poaching investigation. A lot of the guys in the room would have been glad to string up the offenders with no questions asked. Poachers have changed over the last ten or fifteen years. It's no longer a question of some guy out in his back forty taking a deer out of season to stock his larder. Rings have been established, just like drug operations. Their members have no relationship to the land; their only interest is in the money. Short of importing surveillance planes, our biggest hope for catching the local gang was keeping an ear to the ground. Chronic poachers like to brag. They want everyone to know how much smarter they are than the authorities.

I made my way steadily across the room. Les Mills was holding court at a long table set with vises and littered with hooks and feathers, patiently explaining to a novice the intricacies of tying a Royal Coachman. Picking up a beer on my way past the bar, I casually drifted over. I was not sure just what I hoped to accomplish by confronting Les, but his reaction in the bar the other day left me in no doubt that he did, in fact, know something about something. I wanted to find out what. He glanced up, unpleasantly surprised to see me. He scowled. I smiled and lifted my beer bottle in salute. Les's eyes shifted to a point beyond my right shoulder. I saw his head shake fractionally. He made a quick shooing motion with his hands—go away. I was not sure if I was meant to be the recipient of the message, but before I could turn to check, somebody jostled me hard from behind, forcing me off balance and sending my beer bottle crashing to the floor. I turned to glower at the jostler and found myself nose to neck with a dark-haired hulk dressed for the evening in camouflage vest and rolled up sleeves. He sported a dragon tattoo on his right forearm. As I tilted my head back to meet his eyes, I noted that his black moustache needed a trim. So did his nose hairs. I recognized the sartorial splendour of Larry Taylor, Les Mills's grandson. He would be about twenty-two now, I guessed, and he had obviously inherited his size from his father rather than his diminutive mother, Les's daughter. He topped me by a good six inches.

Larry stared at me balefully, his mouth twisted into a sneer. He had a curiously unformed face that still looked more adolescent than mature, as though the features had not yet synthesized with the emerging character. His sterling reputation included vandalism, petty theft, and brawling. He had never held a job for more than a month at a time, his unique talents apparently being better employed in pool halls or blasting around town in a pickup truck, which, in keeping with his understated approach to life, was fitted with monster wheels suitable for mud bog racing. Larry's father had long ago cleared out of town, leaving the boy to be brought up by his pale, apologetic mother and his doting grandfather, both of whom seemed content to spend their lives defending their darling against the slings and arrows of critical public opinion.

Tonight, as usual, he was flanked by his two semi-moronic sidekicks, Daniel and Darryl Pearson, universally dubbed Curly and Moe. To no one's surprise, they called themselves the Stooges, claiming membership in a club whose sole criterion for admittance seemed to be churlish behaviour.

On that basis, I could have tendered my ex-husband's name for consideration, though Nicholas's style had been much more refined. His cultivated exterior had not hinted at the brutishness within, panache rendering his explosive bursts of temper that much more potent. It became clear early in our marriage that what Nicholas wanted was not a wife, but a sycophant. It was a role I was reluctant to fill.

Gradually I had learned what lay at the root of Nicholas's problem. His story of familial dysfunction and abuse was no less pathetic for being unoriginal, but the moral compass with which it had endowed him was so firmly set to self-pity that I felt only a flicker of compassion. The more he raged, the further I withdrew, until the only point of contact left between us was his fist. In those days, I had no idea of how to fight back, but once my arm had been broken I made sure that I learned. Along with firearms instruction, the Ministry requires its COs to take courses in self-defence. Now at least I knew a few basics, and maybe one or two tricks my instructor had taught me outside of class.

Larry Taylor's tone, like his manner, was offensive. "Hey, Charlie," he sneered, "better be a little more careful, eh?" He gestured at the spilled beer. "Don't want to waste our precious natural resources, do ya?" Scattered laughter greeted this witty remark.

I smiled thinly. "Charlie to my friends. Ms. Meikle to you."

Larry reddened. "Who the hell do you think you are,

butch?" His voice rose as he spat out the words. "You're nothin' but a govermint flunky, a fuckin' female bush cop—hasslin' the rest of us while you sit there in your cushy little office collectin' your nice regular paycheck."

I sighed inwardly. Given my job, I'm used to a certain amount of verbal abuse and I seldom bother to respond, but I take exception to personal slurs and I find "butch" particularly wounding. The only pit bull I ever knew was an "it" called Butch and it had to be put down.

Apparently my hard-eyed look lacked force. Larry's flood of invective continued.

"I seen you drivin' around in your little car, wearin' your little uniform. Thinkin' you're some kind of special investigator or somethin'." Larry's eyes narrowed. "Jamesette fuckin' Bond. Alls you do, Charlie, is interfere with people's right to hunt and fish the way they want. The way they need to to survive all the taxes you keep handin' out."

I was used to that one too. By and large people don't differentiate between government departments, or even between the province and the feds. We are all one to Joe Public, tax collectors and petty tyrants. I managed a sympathetic smile. "I guess the sales tax on that new truck you're driving must have been pretty steep, eh Larry? I'm surprised you could afford it."

Larry took a step towards me, fists balled menacingly. I looked at him levelly, smiled again and said nothing. I should have remembered how provocative silence can be.

I was vaguely aware that the floor around us had cleared like morning mist. Larry Taylor was a hotheaded young man spoiling for a fight. But rather than piling on him in a preventative heap, a dozen eager onlookers had formed a ring around us. An out of work no-hoper was going to take out his frustrations on a member of the securely employed middle class. My gender made no difference. The old taboo against hitting women doesn't register with primitives like Larry, who still think we belong in the kitchen or on the back seat of a car, not in positions of authority.

Recent amendments to the gun control laws only exacerbated my position. Hunters who previously enjoyed a comfortable working relationship with their local COs were beginning to grumble about government interference, and the officers themselves, me included, were less than happy about the new requirement to police the region checking up on gun licences. To many of the immediate crowd, I made a legitimate target. I had to hope that calmer heads would eventually prevail and intervene on my behalf.

I was acutely conscious not only of Larry's size, but of his greater expertise with his fists. Most of what I knew about fighting was bluff. In a straight contest, there was no way I was going to win.

I turned and took a couple of steps away, hoping to defuse the bomb by removing the target in a parody of the old slogan, "what if they gave a war and nobody came?" I felt a change in the air behind me, nothing as definite as a noise, but unquestionably a threat. I felt a frisson of the fear I had experienced with Nicholas. I could see from the faces of the onlookers that he was coming for me.

All those useful, and usually dormant, survival

instincts came to my rescue; I was already whipping around to face Larry as he launched himself for the attack. My knee caught him under the rib cage in mid-flight. His breath went out in an audible hiss. Before he could get his bearings, someone grabbed one of his wrists and landed him on his feet with one arm pinned behind him in a nice, painful lock. The audience snickered. I was surprised and gratified to note that it was the staid and sober Geoffrey Purvis, looking every inch the authoritative school principal, who had come to my rescue.

"You bitch," Larry said.

Mr. Purvis gave his arm a little twist and I was pleased to see tears come to his eyes.

"Have you been doing any bear hunting lately, Larry?" I said incautiously.

"Fuck off."

Mr. Purvis twisted again.

From the midst of the watching crowd, Les Mills sprang to his grandson's defence. "Let go of him Geoff!" he shouted, pulling at the principal's restraining arm. "He's just a boy! You've got no call to beat him up over a little spilled beer. Let him go!"

"Spilled beer my ass," I said, looking straight at Les. "You know what this is about as well as I do. And if your boy here is involved in what I think he is, there's a lot more trouble than a bar fight waiting for him."

I nodded to Mr. Purvis, who gave Larry a hard releasing shove in the general direction of Curly and Moe. Les tried to grab his grandson's arm, but Larry shook him off and turned his vindictive face my way. In humiliated fury he shouted, "I'll kill you, Meikle! I swear to God I'll kill you!"

CHAPTER **TEN**

On Friday I stopped by the liquor store for a bottle of wine. Paul and Carole had invited me to dinner. I gathered roast beef was on the menu, so, on the clerk's recommendation, I chose a nice full-bodied red, but I dithered so long over my selection that Young's Hardware was closed by the time I got there. It looked as though I'd be spending another night with the corner of a washcloth wedged into the bathroom faucet.

Two tail-wagging golden retrievers met me at the Ewings's front door: Daisy and Donald, named for the ducks. Behind them, blonde and beautiful, Carole stood smiling a welcome. There was still something of the perky co-ed about Carole, a sort of naive good humour and enthusiasm that had been natural at twenty, but at thirty-five had a forced air. Loss had dulled her original sparkle, but she worked hard to maintain the façade. In unguarded moments, the effort showed in her eyes; most days, her determined cheerfulness seemed the most real part of her.

"Good to see you, Charlie! It's been such a while!" Carole's voice dropped to a lower, more sombre cadence. "Sorry to hear about Jim Griffith." She added a gentle squeeze to her welcoming hug, then pushed me toward the living room while she bore my brown-bagged offering to the kitchen.

"Bring you a drink in a minute," she called over her shoulder.

Paul was already established in front of the fire with the newspaper. Carole breezed in with a glass of scotch on the rocks.

"What's this?" I asked. "Are we moving up from beer?"

"This is a class establishment. We only serve the best. Actually, Paul picked this up at the duty free last time he went to the States. Let me know what you think of it. I'll just get the gravy going." She breezed out again.

Holding my glass aloft to avoid a spill, I fended off Daisy's affectionate advances as I moved to join Paul by the fire. Donald was already comfortably settled by my chair, waiting for me to sit so that he could put his head on my lap. I sat.

Paul grinned at me. "Heard you had a little set-to at the Legion last night. Someone impugn your honour?"

"No. My intelligence."

He laughed. "How so?"

"Les Mills and Larry Taylor . . ."

"Two solid citizens . . ."

". . . are fashioning themselves as the righteous defenders of the little guy against the big bad 'govermint'—the latter being wholly represented by yours truly."

"This is a new approach for them?"

"Actually, it is. They usually spend their time bragging about all the ways they know to beat the system. Maximizing EI benefits, minor tax avoidance schemes. You know. Lately, though, they're both on a kick denouncing government interference in every man's right to make a living off the land. I have been singled out as the human source of the problem."

"Why you?"

"Mm, because of the bears I would think."

"Aha."

"Yes, well, Larry certainly didn't buy that flashy new truck of his on credit."

"Doesn't seem likely," Paul agreed. "You think old Les is in on it with him?"

"No." I stroked Donald's head. Daisy moved over to Paul's chair to demand equal time. "Les certainly knows about the poaching, but he probably figures since it's Larry it's okay, so I should butt out. My bet is the sidekicks, Curly and Moe, are Larry's partners in crime. We have a couple of witnesses who claim to have seen three men, one of whom is a tall guy with a moustache, in the vicinity of the latest carcass. It all fits too well to be anyone else."

"You going to charge them?"

"On what evidence? We've got nothing that will stand up in court. We need to catch them red-handed. But without a twenty-four hour tail on Larry, that's not likely to happen. I'm hoping my little warning last night might cool him off."

Paul looked at me. "From what I heard," he said drily, "it's more likely to send him back out with another target in mind."

"Yeah, well, I think he's only lethal to bears."

"Don't be dumb, Charlie. A hothead with a gun can be just as lethal to people. And I don't think Larry Taylor is the kind to take defeat graciously—especially at the hands of a woman."

"I'll keep my eyes open."

I sipped my drink slowly, savouring the smooth malt

whiskey as it slid over my tongue and down my throat. I thought about the conversation I had had with Ray when I stopped by his garage to pick up my tire.

"I can't repair this, Charlie," he had said, showing me the damage. "This is no simple puncture here. Tire's been slashed." Ray shook his head and clucked like an old hen. "Damn teenagers. I've seen a few of these slashings lately. Must be the 'in' thing to do. Mostly, though, all four tires get the treatment. You were lucky."

I had accepted Ray's explanation at face value this afternoon. Now I didn't feel quite so complacent. Lucky, he had said. Sure I was lucky, if it was random vandalism. But what if it wasn't? What if it was a warning of some kind?

See what I can do to your tire?

Imagine what I could do to you.

Carole came in and perched on the arm of her husband's chair. "What are you two looking so serious about?"

Paul squeezed her knee. "Just trying to talk some sense into Charlie."

"Tough job."

"Thanks a lot," I said. "It's nice to know who your friends really are."

"Maybe you could hire Geoffrey Purvis to be your personal bodyguard," Carole teased. "Or weren't you planning to tell us how he rushed to your rescue like St. George slaying the dragon?"

Paul looked amused. I rolled my eyes. Carole never missed an opportunity to put a romantic spin on even the most unlikely situation, zealous to remind me of what I already knew: not all men are like Nicholas. She had never pried for details, or encouraged any heart-to-heart over the debacle of my marriage, and I was grateful for that. The magnitude of her domestic tragedy reduced mine to mere misadventure. Self-pity would be crass indulgence.

"By the way, Charlie," Carole said, "Paul was telling me about the fish mystery of Finger Lake. Have you had any luck locating the source of the contamination?"

I shook my head. "I didn't get much from the top maps. I thought I might do a little hiking out around the area tomorrow, see if I can turn anything up."

"Alone?" Paul asked.

"Sure, why not?"

Paul looked at me. I looked back. He won. "Feel like taking a little walk with me tomorrow?" I asked resignedly.

The back door slammed and a minor whirlwind blew in in the shape of the Ewings's eleven-year-old son Neil.

"Hey, everybody, I'm home. When do we eat?" Daisy and Donald leapt up to give the boy an enthusiastic welcome. He fussed over them both, shedding jacket and runners as he made his way from kitchen to living room.

"Hey, Charlie, I didn't know you were coming over. You staying for supper? That's great. I have a super new Nintendo game to show you. It's really awesome. When do we eat, anyway?" he asked again, turning to his mother. "I'm starving. Hi Dad."

I watched Neil deliver an animated play by play of the soccer game he had just finished. Paul and Carole gave him their full attention, as they always did. Two years ago, they had lost their daughter Lindsay to leukemia. Her short life had been a rollercoaster of crisis and remission, the kind of stressful ride that can tear a family apart; in their case, it had bound them more tightly together. In the dozen years that I've known them, I've shared in many of their good times, as well as their bad; bridesmaid at their wedding, godmother to their son, I grieved with them through the illness and death of their daughter. I've spent many pleasant evenings like this one in their home, and at times I've envied their closeness. But mostly I'm glad to have my own home to go to at the end of the day. I've never found solitude lonely.

CHAPTER **ELEVEN**

It was about ten the next morning when I stopped by to pick up Paul. Neil came bounding out of the house first. I winced at the sight of his violent orange and purple anorak. We could use it as a beacon, I thought. It would be easily visible to the naked eye at anything up to a five-mile radius. Following closely on his heels were, inevitably, Daisy and Donald. Paul trailed sedately in their wake. He carried two knapsacks.

"One's for Dad's stuff," Neil advised. "But the other one is full of food. I didn't want us to faint with hunger or anything."

"It doesn't look as though there is much to worry about on that score," I said. "Is your mom coming?"

"Nope. Day off, she says. She figures without Dad or me or the dogs around she can really put her feet up for once."

"Smart lady," I said.

I opened the tailgate and the dogs jumped into the car. Neil settled in the back seat, close to the food supplies, and Paul and I got into the front. There was a tape in the deck and it came on as I started the engine. The Nylons were singing golden oldies a cappella.

"Jeez, Charlie," groaned Neil. "Don't you ever listen to any real music?"

"It's this or nothing."

"Well, nothing is better than that."

"I agree," I said, smiling.

Neil made a face in the mirror. "You know what I meant."

I turned off the back speakers. Neil gave me a thumb and forefinger okay.

"Where are we headed?" Paul asked.

"Finger Lake," I said. "We might as well start at the identifiable end of the problem and try to work our way to the source. We can park at Jim Griffith's. I have to have a look around the place anyway, to make sure everything is okay. His executor, Laura Rhodes, wants to sell the place sooner or later. Preferably sooner, I'd guess."

"Is she not exactly the outdoor type?"

"Hardly. She thinks a spinning reel is something pioneers used for winding wool."

"It's not surprising, then, that she never made Geddes Lake her vacation destination."

"No, but now she feels guilty that she didn't make the effort."

"Yeah, well, I guess guilt and grief go hand in hand pretty often."

I winced at the bitterness in his voice. I knew he was thinking about Lindsay. He had met his daughter's death with a cold despair that was frightening, and I wondered sometimes if he found her loss easier, or harder, to bear in the face of Carole's resolute vivacity.

Daisy and Donald were practically jumping out of their skins by the time we arrived at the cabin, so Paul took them down to the water to retrieve sticks, while Neil and I headed inside. Neil made a beeline for the kitchen, though I'd already told him there was nothing there. I could hear him rummaging through cupboards while I checked the screens on the windows and made sure the generator was shut down. A whoop of triumph from Neil startled me into banging my elbow on the doorjamb. Through clenched teeth I was asking the age-old question, why they call it a funny bone, when Neil appeared carrying a jar of what looked like water with a glob of clay in the bottom.

"Look at this! What would Mr. Griffith use this for?"

I eyed the jar suspiciously. "Where did you find that?"

"In the back of a cupboard, behind a bunch of paper towels. What d'you think it is?"

I took the jar from his hand and twisted the lid, which came off easily. I sniffed at the gloopy mixture.

"It's not food," I said.

Neil gave me a look. "I know I can't eat it Charlie, but what is it?"

I frowned. "It looks like . . . tailings." Gently, I stirred the water, watching grey particles rise to swirl in the eddy created by my finger.

"What're tailings?"

"Well, garbage, really," I said. "In a mine that produces ore, like gold, they have to crush up a lot of rock before the sorters can extract the metal." Neil nodded.

"So all the part that isn't gold, is garbage, and it gets thrown out. That's what the tailings are."

"Where do they put 'em?"

"What—the tailings?" I screwed the lid back onto the jar. "It depends what kind of operation it is. Some produce dry tailings, most companies bury it all under water."

"Well that sounds better than leaving heaps of dirt all over the place."

I smiled. "Out of sight, out of mind? The problem is, the tailings produce acid."

"Like pollution?"

"Exactly."

"What I don't get is, why would Mr. Griffith keep a jar of tailings in his kitchen cupboard?"

From outside the cabin, came a flurry of barking. We stepped onto the porch to see what was going on. Daisy and Donald were venting their outrage at a squirrel that had outwitted them and now sat scolding from the safety of a tree.

"They got tired of water sports," Paul said. "Are you two about ready to go?"

I set the jar on Jim's desk and locked the door, wondering, like Neil, what mine tailings could possibly be doing in the cabin in the first place.

According to the top maps, the land gradually sloped downward from Windrush Mine to Finger Lake. That meant our outward journey would be uphill; the way back would be easy. Neil and the dogs acted as trail blazers, crashing through the underbrush ahead of us. From time to time we caught a glimpse of Neil's brilliant jacket. It made him easy to follow.

We did not pursue a straight-line course, but tracked back and forth looking, unsuccessfully, for clues. We found plenty of evidence of animal activity. The deer, which spend a lot of time around the rivers and lakes feeding on water plants during the summer, were now beginning to move back into the woods for fall and winter forage. We spotted a pair near a little clearing. The doe's reddish summer hair was gradually giving way to a darker blue winter coat. Most of the fawn's spots had disappeared. The buck was probably out looking for trouble.

We kept up a steady pace. The day was clear and still warm, the trail not difficult to follow. It had been years since I had done any real trekking. Still, I was a long way from the curse of "city muscles" accustomed only to level pavement. City muscles tire easily on constantly changing trails, where every step is a matter of balance.

About an hour after our starting out, a shout from Neil heralded our arrival at the Windrush mine. A skeletal head frame loomed over the top of the rise, the gothic water tower and long, box-shaped mill standing gaunt against the still lush backdrop of woods. In front of the buildings, the ground had been cleared for heavy equipment; surprisingly little had grown back since the mine closed down. Truck tire tracks were still clearly visible in the dirt. To the left, a small mountain of tailings squatted like a toad in a malodorous pond.

"Oh, man, is this place ever cool," Neil enthused. "Can't you just picture Freddy Krueger hanging out here waiting for his next victim?"

"It's the first thought that came to my mind, all right," I said. Turning to Paul I added, "What are you teaching this kid?"

"Hey, I'm just his father. I'm not responsible."

"Can we eat now?" Neil demanded. "I'm starved."

We unpacked the food and prepared to picnic in that unlovely spot. Carole had organized the rations with

Neil's assistance, so there was plenty of peanut butter to balance the corned beef, and lots of cookies. The Ewings drank pop. I unzipped my own knapsack and took out my trusty thermos. All that exercise had me crying out for caffeine. The dogs kept a close eye on the proceedings, ever alert for a fallen crumb.

Through a mouthful of sandwich Neil asked, "What are we here for exactly?"

"That's hard to say, exactly," Paul answered. "We're looking for anything that could be contaminating the water in Finger Lake."

"Like tailings?"

Paul looked at his son in surprise. "What do you know about tailings?"

I explained about the jar Neil had found at Jim's cabin.

"We can pick it up on the way back, and maybe you could have a look at it at the lab?"

Paul nodded.

"To get back to your question Neil, there's been no outward sign of any problem between here and the lake— at least, none that we noticed. So the plan is to look around here a little . . ."

"If we can," I interrupted.

"What do you mean if we can?" Neil demanded. "What's to stop us?"

"Well, little things mostly. Like laws against trespass. Locks on doors." I shrugged.

"Huh." He gathered up the wrappings from his sandwich and stuffed them into the knapsack. "When do we start?"

"As soon as I finish my coffee."

Neil rolled his eyes. "That could be forever. Mind if I start without you?"

"Be my guest."

He whistled for the dogs and they started a great circle tour of the head frame. Paul watched them go.

"He's a great kid," I said.

Paul nodded. "You got any coffee to spare?" He held out a plastic mug and as I filled it with what remained in the thermos, he said, "Are you going to tell me about it?"

"Tell you about what?"

"Whatever it is that's bugging you. It's not just the lake water, and it's not Larry Taylor."

I sighed and said, "I'm having trouble buying into the accidental death theory."

Paul stared at me. "You mean Jim Griffith?"

"Of course. Who else?"

"I had no idea there was any question of its being anything other than an accident. Are the police investigating it?"

"No." I studied my boot.

After a few moments, Paul cleared his throat. "Would you mind telling me just what the hell you're talking about?"

I told him. I told him about the tackle on the dock, the little boat drifting in the lake, the lifejacket still hanging on the peg behind the door. Paul was as skeptical as Laura had been.

"There is no way Jim would have set off to go fishing without that lifejacket," I argued. "And saying he meant to go back for it is ludicrous. If he planned to go back to the cabin, he certainly wouldn't have untied the lines to his boat before going. It makes no sense in the first place for a seasoned fisherman like him to have cast off his boat when all his gear was still lying on the dock. The whole scenario stinks."

"Huh. And what about the scenario you're suggesting? If Jim's death wasn't an accident, then what was it? Murder?"

I didn't answer.

Paul persisted. "That's what you're saying, isn't it? That Jim Griffith was murdered? Who would have done that, for God's sake? Who the hell would have any reason to murder a perfectly nice old guy like Jim? It's not as if he had anything worth stealing. There wasn't anything missing from his cabin, was there?"

"No," I admitted.

"Then what?" Paul made an open-handed gesture of exasperation. "Jesus, Charlie, if there's no motive, how can you begin to think there might have been a murder? Talk about something not making any sense. Have you mentioned any of this to the police? Or even to the coroner? Or, God forbid, to the poor guy's executor?"

I said, "No, I haven't told the police. For all the reasons that you just mentioned. But I knew Jim Griffith. And the picture I saw when I found his body . . ." I shrugged, ". . . is wrong, somehow. I know it is."

"You know." Paul shook his head. "And what does Ms. Rhodes think? Presumably she knew the guy pretty well herself. What does she have to say about it?"

"What makes you think I told her?"

"I'm psychic."

"Yeah, well, she thinks I'm nuts, too."

"So what are you going to do?"

"Oh, hell, Paul, I don't know. Just keep poking around, I guess. Maybe eventually something will turn up."

The dogs came racing back, tails wagging, tongues lolling. Neil drooped dejectedly behind.

"Find anything?"

"Nah, there's nothing going on here," his tone was disgusted.

"Freddy wasn't lurking about anywhere?"

"Gimme a break, Charlie."

I laughed. Reshouldering our knapsacks, we wandered down for a look at the tailings pond. The Windrush tailings looked like tailings anywhere, including the jar on Jim's desk. Paul had come prepared to collect samples for analysis.

Leaving him to scoop muck into vials, I moved over to inspect the door of the head frame. It was locked, with a brand new lock. I looked it over carefully. Sometimes new locks can be stiff, difficult to close securely. Someone must have had trouble with this one. It took only a little pressure to force it open.

"Where did you learn that trick?" Paul asked over my shoulder.

"I watch a lot of movies."

"Right." His tone was dry. "Just don't tell Neil. All I need is for my son to become a break-and-enter expert."

"Hey, cool, this door was open, huh?" Neil had arrived with the dogs.

The portal opened onto a spiral shaft that did not extend very deeply into the rock. The Windrush Mine had been built on a rich vein of ore discovered fairly close to the surface. Excited speculators had hailed it as the mother lode of the century, sure that the initial find was a harbinger of untold riches waiting to be tapped. In time, overwhelming optimism gave way to mundane acceptance of the limitations of the find. Still, the Windrush had provided steady employment to three generations of Geddes Lakers before being shut down.

It was dark inside the head frame, darker still down the shaft. The air was surprisingly damp and fetid; it held a faint chemical odour I couldn't immediately identify. Benzine, maybe. But in a mine shaft?

Pulling my flashlight out of my knapsack I flicked a look at Neil, hovering in the doorway with the dogs, then at Paul, who had already reached the same decision.

"We'll wait outside," he said.

"Aw Dad, come on," Neil whined in protest.

"I need a lookout," I said. "Let me know if you see anyone coming." Neil made a face.

Sketching a small salute I turned into the shaft. I played the beam of my flashlight over the ceiling, walls, and floor, orienting myself, gauging the space. Slowly I moved forward, feet squelching in the muck, the smell growing stronger as I advanced. I was pretty sure I wasn't going to like what I found.

I rounded the bend in the shaft cautiously and came face to face with an ecological disaster. The place was full of oil drums, some rusting, several improperly sealed, with stuff trickling down their sides. None of the drums was labelled, but I was willing to bet they did not contain natural herbs and spices.

Here and there small pools of water reflected the light.

Clearly the shaft was flooding, not an uncommon occurrence in a disused mine. Equally clearly, however, the shaft was not filling up. Somewhere the water was percolating through fissures in the rock into the groundwater, taking whatever chemicals were oozing from the drums with it. The natural incline of the land would inevitably carry the resulting brew down to the nearest reservoir, Finger Lake.

CHAPTER **TWELVE**

Sunday morning was a memory by the time I dragged myself down to the kitchen to scramble some eggs. The coffee was on a timer I had forgotten to turn off the night before and had been brewing since seven o'clock, which made it too thick even for me. I dumped it out and started a new pot.

I don't usually sleep much past seven, but Saturday's *Night Owl Theatre* was a Bogart triple hitter I couldn't resist: *The African Queen*, *Key Largo*, and *Casablanca*. I watched Bogey charm three of the all-time great ladies of the silver screen and wished I'd been one of them.

The weather was a dismal repeat of the previous weekend. Moodily, I shuffled into the living room and flipped on the TV, hoping to catch the midday news. An attractive anchorwoman with an insincere smile was just wrapping up a story about native land claims in British Columbia. She spoke of "ties to nature" and to illustrate her point, she described the Kwakiutl tribe's belief that when a salmon was caught and eaten, its soul returned to salmon country. The Indians were careful, she said, not to destroy its bones. They were afraid that if the bones were burnt, the soul of the fish would be lost and the salmon would be unable to return to the tribe the following year.

The newswoman's patronizing tone irritated me; there was more to her bit of folklore than quaint superstition.

The Kwakiutl revered the fish they caught because fish was their chief source of food. They were not slow to note that there is a direct link between many fish and full stomachs and no fish and empty stomachs. Belief may be theoretical, but there is nothing abstract about starvation. It is one of nature's more obvious laws that you can't afford to be sloppy with the things that keep you alive.

Nor, I thought, with the things that can kill you.

I spent some time trying to piece together the scattered bits of information I had accumulated about the toxic waste at Windrush. I knew I would have to report my discovery to the appropriate higher agencies and allow them to follow their politically correct procedures in cleaning up. But, I persuaded myself, technically I represented an appropriate government agency. It was eminently reasonable that I should carry out some preliminary investigations myself.

I reviewed what I had to date, concluding ruefully that it wasn't much. However sure I might be that the grunge being stored at the Windrush Mine was responsible for the failing fish population at Finger Lake, I would have to wait for Paul's findings to confirm it. It was up to him to identify the chemicals we had found in the shaft. Then we would see if we could find any trace of them in the Finger Lake fish or in the tailings from the jar in Jim's cabin. Without that linkage, all I had was a case of unauthorized dumping.

At ten o'clock the next morning, I was combing through records at the Geddes Lake Town Hall, trying to determine who owned the Windrush Mine. My ruminations the day before had suggested this line of inquiry as a good jumping off point, but after two hours of pawing through dry legalese, all I had uncovered was a series of numbered holding companies. No names, no one to point a finger at, no leads on the source of the toxic waste being stored in the mine.

I stopped at Dot's for a quick fix to my flagging spirits and then headed back to the office. The usual quiet pandemonium reigned. Joan gestured to me wildly to pick up line two. It was Mrs. Creighton again, the old lady on the Windrush Mine road who objected to blaspheming tire changers.

Chuckling, I took the phone, saying, "What's the problem, ma'am? More midnight madness out your way?" and immediately regretted my tone. The old lady's distress carried clearly down the line.

"It's Luther. My dog. He's been hurt." I could hear the tears in her voice. "I found him down the road about an hour ago. He often goes out on the prowl in the morning. Right after breakfast." She sobbed. "Always comes back around eleven. For tea. Well, he doesn't drink tea, of course, he has water and some biscuits . . ."

"Mrs. Creighton," I said, gently, hoping to prod her back to the point. She cleared her throat.

"He didn't come back this morning. Even when I called him, he didn't come. Luther always comes when I call. He's a good dog."

"Mrs. Creighton," I hesitated, "is Luther badly hurt?"

She was crying openly now. "He's dead. And he looks," her voice broke on the words, "he looks like he's been mauled."

I shook off the image that word brought to mind.

"Mrs. Creighton," I said firmly, "I want you to go and make yourself a cup of tea. Put lots of sugar in it. Drink it. I'll be right over."

I broke all speed limits getting there. The Windrush Mine Road ran west out of town, shabby warehouses and light industry gradually giving way to pine forest and a sprinkling of cottages spread at intervals along the river. About five miles down the road, maybe a mile east of the mine itself, I turned into the drive where "Creighton" had been freshly painted in yellow on a black mailbox. The small log house beyond looked warmly attractive, the golden hue of the wood accented by window boxes full of late blooming mums. A flagstone path wound past Christmas pine to a wide covered porch where a rocking chair sat angled to the water. I knocked on the door. It took the occupant a long time to respond. I was just lifting my hand to knock again, when the door opened to reveal a tiny elderly woman, leaning heavily on a cane. Her thinning grey hair was still long enough to be swept into a coil on top of her head, giving her an air of style and dignity at odds with the shabby cardigan and old jeans she wore.

"Mrs. Creighton?"

She nodded mutely, half turning to gesture me inside. To the right of the entrance was an immaculate sitting room. I glimpsed a mantel littered with photographs, most of them of dogs. Mrs. Creighton followed my gaze and her faded blue eyes filled with tears. Gently I took her elbow and steered her toward the fireplace. She moved stiffly, gripping her cane tightly in her right hand, sinking bonelessly into her chair. I guessed she had not taken my advice about the tea. Hastily I searched for a bottle of brandy, on the grounds that people who claimed it had medicinal qualities knew what they were talking about. If you've had a bad shock, drink brandy. Feeling queasy? Drink brandy. Suffering from green shivers and cold shakes? Drink brandy.

There was a bottle on the kitchen shelf. I poured a healthy shot and held the glass while she drank. Gradually the stiffness eased from her body and she revived like a wilting flower after rain.

"You've given me cooking brandy, young woman," she said tartly. "The drinking brandy is over there." She indicated a pine icebox.

"My apologies," I smiled. "I'm Charlie Meikle."

"Charlie?"

"Well, Charlotte, actually."

"Yes," Mrs. Creighton said, looking me over. "The young woman on the phone." She paused. You'll have to help me bury Luther, Charlie. I can't manage him alone."

"Where is he?"

"Down the road about a quarter of a mile. Left hand side. I covered him as best I could."

She had marked the place with fallen branches. Kneeling, I brushed aside the leaves to stare at the savaged body of a once beautiful Irish setter. A flattened path dotted by dried gobbets of blood was pathetic evidence of how far he had dragged himself. He had been trying to get home. I had a vivid mental image of an old lady limping down the dirt road in search of her slaughtered pet and felt that I could do with a shot of brandy myself.

We buried Luther under a stand of blazing yellow

larch. Mrs. Creighton insisted that I stay to tea, which she served, surprisingly, in fine china mugs, accompanied by thin slices of buttered bread.

"I've always had dogs, you know," she said, gesturing to the collection of canine pictures. "They make wonderful companions. Totally uncritical in their affections." Something in her tone implied an experience with humans that was less than satisfactory.

She looked at me. "What would have done that to Luther? A wolf?"

I was doubtful. "It would be unusual around here. There are bears in the neighbourhood, but for one to attack a dog . . ." I shook my head. "I'll have a look around, see what kind of tracks I can find."

Mrs. Creighton nodded. "You'll let me know?" She glanced again at the grinning doggy face framed on the table beside her.

"I'll let you know."

Armed with my gun and a soup bone from Mrs. Creighton's larder, I followed the bloodied path back through the brush. The scene of the fight was easy to locate. Grass and small bushes had been trampled in an uneven circle about a metre wide. Tufts of red gold hair clung to the gorse. Poor Luther had died hard.

I searched for wolf spoor and found only dog droppings. Canine tracks in the mud led off in the direction of the Windrush Mine. Well, well, I thought, maybe someone has invested in something more than new locks.

As quietly as I could I made my way to the clearing across from the mine. A black van with red markings I couldn't read was parked near the entrance to the shaft, the same entrance I had used only a couple of days ago. The door stood ajar, but I could see no sign of activity and, fool that I was, I decided to move in for a closer look.

I had taken no more than a step when a low growl sounded to my right. I whirled to face Luther's killer.

He was as big as a wolf and of similar colouring, probably a shepherd cross of some kind. It was clear that he planned to attack.

But I had a plan too.

The dog crouched, ready to spring, waiting only for me to make the first move. I was armed with a gun, but I knew that in the time it would take me to unbuckle my holster, draw, and fire, the animal would be on me, tearing my throat out. The dog quivered, haunches tensing for the jump.

I felt the weight of the soup bone in my hand and I hurled it underhand as far as I could, banking heavily on the fact that canine intelligence has some limitations, whereas canine greed has none. The dog went for it.

I went for my gun.

Before I could even unclip my holster I felt a crashing pain on the back of my head and dropped like a stone.

CHAPTER **THIRTEEN**

I spat out a mouthful of dirt and tried to sit up, which was a serious mistake. My head felt better on the ground.

I lay without moving for uncountable grey minutes and eventually the pain eased enough for me to take stock of my position. Apart from my pounding head, I didn't feel any unusual soreness. All my limbs were still attached, and my clothing seemed to be intact. My right hand rested loosely on top of my gun. That puzzled me. I didn't remember drawing my weapon but if I had, it should have been in my left hand.

Carefully, I levered myself into a sitting position, and waited for my head to stop whirling and my eyes to focus. Ten feet away, the killer dog lay peacefully on his side, all savagery erased by the bullet in his massive chest. Apparently, I had shot the attacking animal before— what? Fainting with fright? Ah, no, there was a handy tree root. I must have tripped just as the gun went off. Lucky I'm such an ace shot. I shook my head, regretted it immediately, and wondered why anyone had bothered to set up the scenario. The whole thing looked stagey, like something from an old movie.

I felt weak and nauseated. For a minute, I panicked over the thought of a fractured skull, but decided it was more likely concussion. Dragging myself to my feet, I turned my head carefully in the direction of the mine.

The van was gone. I reholstered my gun.

It was a long, weary trudge back to Mrs. Creighton's cabin. When at last I stumbled to her door, she greeted me with gratifying concern, pushing me into the same chair she had occupied a few hours earlier, and handing me a glass of non-cooking brandy from the appropriate cabinet. I sank back in the chair with my eyes closed while Mrs. Creighton's homey clatterings in the kitchen gradually succeeded the dance troupe in my head. Eventually, the combined smells of rich stew and baking bread roused me from my stupor. Mrs. Creighton placed a tray on my lap, then settled herself in the chair opposite. We ate in companionable silence.

"Delicious," I said, sponging up the last drop of thick broth with a piece of brown bread.

My hostess nodded pleased acknowledgement of the compliment. "That's an original recipe. I made it up when my husband and I first started coming here, over fifty years ago. We ate a lot of 'make do' meals in those days, while the mine was still being developed. Then, of course, the money started to roll in and we more than made do."

"Your husband was involved with the Windrush Mine?"

"Oh, yes. Ben was one of the original shareholders. This," she made a sweeping gesture, "was just a one room cabin when we started out. Everything, but everything, we had went into the development of that mine. When it paid off, we built a big house in the Ottawa valley. Raised two boys. Kept the cabin and built it up for holidays and fishing trips. The boys loved it. Then Ben sold out his shares in the Windrush." Her mouth twisted in an ironic smile. "And developed new interests."

I looked the question. She nodded ruefully, but there was an undertone of humour in her voice when she said, "It can happen to the best of us."

She was not the kind of woman to let bitterness diminish her. Once past the initial shock, she would have dealt with the pain of her husband's defection with much the same practicality that she had shown over the death of her dog.

"The boys?" I asked.

"My boys were already grown and leading their own lives. If things had gone well for Ben, maybe I would have gone on to do something else in my life as well. But just about a year after he left me, Ben was diagnosed with cancer. He took a long time dying and long before it was over the little secretary lost interest. She took off with most of Ben's money and all of his pride. I brought him back up here. Looked after him until he died." She gave a little shrug. "What else could I do?"

I could think of several things, but I realized that Irene Creighton would not have considered any of them an option. She was a lady of the old school. Ben Creighton had been a fool, I thought.

"Don't you find it lonely, living here all by yourself now?" I asked.

She shook her head. "I'm ready to be alone," she said, but a note of pain disturbed the even tenor of her voice and brought us abruptly back to my reason for being there. I wondered what it had cost her to wait until I'd recovered a bit before asking about her beloved pet. "You found out what attacked Luther."

I told her what had happened to me outside the mine. She shook her head over my description of the offending dog; she had never seen it in the area before. The fact that I had come to with my gun in the wrong hand produced more of a reaction.

"Was your gun actually fired?"

"Yeah. One bullet."

"So an objective observer would have thought that you had in fact shot the dog and tripped and knocked yourself out."

"God, I hope people don't think I'm that much of a klutz," I said indignantly.

She chuckled, and poured us both some coffee. "What I don't understand is, why the person who hit you didn't kill you outright? Or let the dog do it?"

I choked on the coffee. "Don't sugar coat it, Mrs. C., just tell me exactly what you think."

That earned me a sharp response. As though I were a recalcitrant child, she said, "Don't play parlour games. If you want me to butt out, say so. If not, let's put our cards on the table and see if we can make some sense out of all this."

I wanted to hug her. She listened without interruption for almost an hour while I told her rather disjointedly about Jim Griffith's death, about the problems at Finger Lake, about the apparent link to the Windrush Mine, and even about my conviction that Larry Taylor must be responsible for all the recent bear poaching. She was inclined to agree with me on that point.

"I've known that boy most of his life. His father worked for Ben at the Windrush at one time. Lorne

Taylor always took the easy way out. No staying power. I wasn't surprised when he left town. As for Larry, he's been spoiled by his grandfather since he was a child. The mother's not very strong-willed; the boy could always bully her. Had a vicious streak a mile wide. I can see him poaching bears and enjoying it, and I don't mean just the money aspect. I think you're wrong, though, if you figure he slashed your tire. It would be more like him to wreck the whole vehicle. One little tire would hardly satisfy him. No, I think that was probably done by his Grandpa Les."

"Les!" I said in astonishment.

She nodded. "Oh, yes. Les has spent a good part of his life trying to protect that boy, and my guess is he wanted to keep you from confronting him. So he tried to stop you getting to that meeting. It's the kind of thing a weasel like Les would do."

Avoidance was clearly not one of Mrs. Creighton's personal coping strategies.

"I'm no scientist," she went on, "so I wouldn't presume to comment on the Finger Lake problem, but I can tell you one thing that might help. Your friend Jim Griffith was no stranger to the Windrush Mine. He was involved with it for at least twenty-five years." Mrs. Creighton paused for effect. When she was sure she had my full attention, she said, "He was the company auditor."

CHAPTER **FOURTEEN**

I phoned Laura first thing in the morning, but got only voice mail at both numbers she had given me. I left a message at her office.

At my own office, things were slightly hilarious. The other two COs, Jeff Haley and Bob Morrison, had spent the night staking out the fishing hole at Manitou Creek. Officially, lake trout season ends on September 30th, but there are always deadbeats who won't follow the rules. Field officers work a lot of evenings and weekends— that's when the poachers are out and the licensed hunters and fishermen are doing their thing. Jeff, Bob, and I work it on a rotating schedule. It had been their turn last night.

A small knot of people was gathered around them like spectators at a tennis match, listening with amusement as they bounced the story back and forth.

"So I park my car about 100 yards from the bridge," Jeff was saying. "Tuck it nicely into the bush. Inconspicuous as all get out. After about half an hour, along comes this truck. Two guys jump out with nets and spears and head down to the water. Third guy stays in the truck as a lookout. Every so often, he gets out to fire a beer can down the bank and crack open another one."

He paused and Bob took over the story. "Jeff calls me on the radio. I drive over and block the road into the creek with my car. There's a high bank on one side, a tree on the other. Absolutely no way around me. This looks like the easiest bust in the world, right? We're talking about a dead end road, guys with illegal gear fishing out of season. All we have to do is wait for them to get back to the truck with the fish and we've got all three of them. A gift." He shook his head in disbelief. "So I sit there in the dark for twenty minutes, lights off, waiting, and finally Jeff is on the radio again."

"I tell him the two guys have come up the bank, thrown their gear into the back of the truck, and are on their way," Jeff went on.

Bob nodded. "I see the glow of lights coming around the corner. Just as the truck pulls into view, I flash on the red light. Driver stops. I move ahead a little. He starts to back up. Jeff's headlights are coming up behind him, so he stops again. Jeff and I both get out and start walking towards him. Just as we get to the truck, he throws it into reverse and floors it. I don't know what the hell he thought he was doing. Jeff jumps out of the way, this guy goes straight back off the road and smashes into a tree. Tree limb breaks off and lands on top of his hood. Bam! Right on top. Guy's buddies are screaming at him. Guy's laughing like a maniac. We get to the car, rip open the door and there he sits, beer in hand. Looks up at us with this stupid grin on his face and says, "How'd you like that? Didn't spill a drop."

The laughter that greeted the punchline was interrupted by the shrilling of the phone. It was Laura, returning my call.

"Charlie. I just got in and got your message. I meant to phone you today anyway to see how things are going. I really appreciate your helping me out like this."

"No problem," I said. "How about a little quid pro quo?"

A pause. "You want some free legal advice?"

I laughed. "Not exactly. I want some information about Jim Griffith. Specifically about his connection with the Windrush Mine. I understand he was the mine auditor at one point."

"Oh, yes, for about twenty-five years. That's how he got to know the Geddes Lake area in the first place. He used to go up there on a fairly regular basis and he liked it so much, he bought that cabin there when he retired. Why do you ask?"

"The day he died, Jim left a message that he wanted to see me about something."

"I remember. You seemed to think that was significant. Have you found out what the something was?"

"Yes, I have and it seems to be linked to the Windrush Mine. Unfortunately, I'm having a lot of trouble finding out anything about the current ownership of the mine and I think that's where I need to go from here. Got any suggestions?"

"Maybe one or two." Laura paused. "Are you planning to fill me in on the whole story or are you looking for professional services only?"

"Mm, well, most of what I have so far is conjecture."

"You're skating," she said. "Tell me this, does any of your conjecture relate to Jim's death?"

"Yeah I think so, but . . ." Silence filled the line. Maybe I was being overly cautious. On the other hand, I had very few facts. If I was right and there was more to Jim Griffith's death than simple accident, I wanted to be able to give Laura complete answers to the inevitable questions of why and how. Better by far to tell her I'd made a mistake than leave her dangling.

Her next comment made me wonder if I'd spoken out loud. "Whether it's the full story or not, I think I have a right to know what you've found out, Charlie," she said. "In lawyer talk, it's called disclosure."

I gave in. "Okay, you win. I'm willing to make a deal. You find out who's in charge at Windrush and I'll fill you in on what I know."

"And what you think," she pressed.

I sighed. "And what I think."

"Deal. Give me a couple of days. I'll call you Friday."

"Why don't we schedule a conference instead? I haven't been to the big city for a while and I've been offered a free ride this weekend."

"Okay, sounds good. You need a place to stay?"

"No thanks, just directions on how to find you."

"Take a cab."

CHAPTER **FIFTEEN**

Paul dropped by my office on Wednesday. His report was frightening. The drums being stored at the Windrush mine held a whole compendium of different chemicals. They must have come from a variety of sources; no single industry would produce that kind of diverse mix.

For obvious reasons, the storing of toxic chemicals is very closely regulated. But it is also a very expensive undertaking. This would not be the first time a company had opted to cut costs and try to hide its garbage in a self-designated storage site. That was risky enough when a single chemical was involved. But here we were talking about the equivalent of a toxic soup. Who knew what the cumulative effects of all these chemicals mixing together would be? What other as yet unseen damage was occurring was anybody's guess. For me the big question was, where had it all come from?

Paul was still talking. "I'll need to collect some tissue samples, Charlie. None of that junk in the drums is naturally occurring. If I can prove the existence of some of those same chemicals in the Finger Lake fish, we've got a real case."

I didn't answer him right away. It was a fair guess that someone had gone big time into the lucrative sideline of toxic waste disposal. There was no shortage of buyers in that particular market. Plenty of companies would be more than happy to hand over their garbage to the lowest bidder, no questions asked. Jim Griffith had obviously reached a similar conclusion. Given his intimate knowledge of the Windrush, it seemed probable that he had contacted someone connected with the mine to confront them with his evidence. I wished he had called me first, because I was pretty sure that whoever he had talked to, had decided to ensure that he did not talk to anyone else.

Paul noticed my hesitation and had no trouble at all diagnosing its cause. He said flatly, "You'll be in shit up to your ears if you try to make the call on this alone, Charlie. There is no way you can handle a mess like this one by yourself. And the Ministry sure as hell can't stick it on the back burner while you play private investigator."

I waved him off. "I have no intention of delaying the clean up. God knows, with the amount of muck that has already leached into the aquifer, it may never get cleaned up. But you know the likelihood of anyone else believing Jim's death was more than an accident. You don't believe it yourself." His expression told me I had scored a point. "And, you know as well as I do that once the bureaucratic yahoos get hold of this, the only thing that is going to matter a damn to them is the amount of political mileage they can get out of pointing fingers and pulling long faces for the television cameras."

Paul studied me in silence for a long, considering moment. I stared right back. Finally he sighed, "I hate to see you out there on that limb all by yourself, Charlie. You have a lousy sense of balance." He smiled ruefully. "I guess you've got yourself a spotter."

I didn't stop to evaluate why it was so important to me

to prove my theory about Jim's death. Maybe it had something to do with my father's death so many years ago and my unwillingness then and now to meekly accept fate's accidents, but I didn't want to waste time on an analysis of my motivations. I had set myself a task and I would do my best to see it through.

First though, I'd help Paul collect his samples.

Electrofishing can be done at any time. Spring is the best season for sampling, when adults and young mingle in warmer inshore waters. But fall is probably the next best time; adult fish tend to move back toward shore again as the lake water cools. And evening, when the predators move in to feed, is most productive. Paul and I arrived at Finger Lake at dusk.

I donned a life jacket and hip waders, then strapped on the weatherproof, metallic backpack that housed the shocker. Looking like a hick spaceman with a butterfly net, I waded along the shoreline, choosing my spot. Any kind of cover, submerged brush or trees, has a concentrating effect on fish distribution. I moved carefully around the little cove at the eastern end of the lake. A slow, deliberate capture style is a whole lot safer than fish chasing, and it yields more representative samples. In this case we weren't gathering statistical data on species or population abundance and structure. We weren't planning to stun the fish; we were going for the kill.

The batteries and generators we needed carry more than enough current to electrocute a person. I wondered what it would be like to feel that much shock going through you. Would the brain have time to register pain, or would sensation be immediately arrested, as breathing and heartbeat jolted to a stop? I hoped I'd never find out.

We drove back to town in full dark and parted company at the Ministry building.

"I'll just go in and put these guys on ice until tomorrow," Paul said, gesturing at the fish. "Feel like coming by for supper?"

I shook my head. "Not tonight, thanks. I've got some stuff to do before I go to Toronto."

"Do me a favour Charlie, will you?"

"Sure. What?"

"Take it easy. Don't do anything stupid."

I raised an eyebrow at him.

"If you're right about Jim, you're dealing with a murderer. You need any help, you call me."

"I'll be careful," I said. "And thanks."

He smiled, saluted, and turned away into the building. I climbed into my car and drove home.

The place was dark when I pulled into the driveway. I must have forgotten to set the timer for the lights again. Damn, I hate going into a dark, empty house. As I fitted the key in the lock, my foot brushed against something lying across the threshold. I squinted at it, but couldn't tell what it was until I reached inside the door and flipped on the outside light.

It was a rat. A big one. It had been sliced open along the length of its belly, and lay, legs splayed, guts spilling over the doorframe. Blood pooled under and around it. My stomach heaved.

Grabbing some heavy gloves and a shovel from the garage, I quickly dug a hole at the edge of the woods and buried the thing. Then I hosed down the doorway and sprinkled it with bleach.

Inside, I turned on all the lights and the television, trying to banish the stark, sickening image of the rat and replace it with the bright, mindless faces of the people on the screen. I took a healthy shot of brandy; it was becoming quite a habit with me. The phone trilled on the table behind me. Absently I turned to pick it up.

"Hello."

Muffled whispers, then, "Did you get the message, animal lover? Now you know what happens to rats. They get exterminated."

The phone went dead. I stared at the receiver in my hand. The cornball dialogue would almost have been funny were it not for the mutilated animal on my doorstep. That was the work of one very sick mind. I thought I knew whose. On my way out, I slammed the door so hard the windows rattled. It was childish, but it made me feel better, and I suspect it saved Les Mills from a broken nose when I got to his house.

CHAPTER **SIXTEEN**

Les's daughter opened the door of her white stucco house to reveal a painfully clean hallway. Dorrie Taylor was a pale, indefinite woman with the same look of reproachful acceptance a dog has when it senses another blow about to descend. She recognized trouble when it came knocking.

"I'm looking for Larry, Mrs. Taylor," I said with a polite smile. She wasn't fooled.

With pained resignation she asked, "What's he done now?" There was no resonance at all in her voice. Larry's mother had paid regularly over the years for her son's mistakes: from broken windows to smashed-up cars, an out-of-court settlement on an assault charge once, and bail more than once. Looking at Dorrie Taylor's haggard face, I thought the financial tab was probably the least of it.

"Could I speak to him, please?" I repeated.

This was obviously a departure from the norm. People generally went out of their way to avoid talking to Larry Taylor. It was much easier by far to simply present the bill for whatever havoc he had wrought to his mother. I felt like a shit adding to her burden of guilt over her son. This was one bill, I thought grimly, that he was going to pay himself.

"I don't . . ." Mrs. Taylor began uncertainly. "He's not . . ." She looked vaguely around, seeking inspiration from the floral print wallpaper and not finding it. Her thin voice called out, "Dad?"

"What's going on there, Dorrie? Who's that at the door?" Les appeared in the hallway holding a beer can in one hand while busily hitching up his pants with the other. The look of mild irritation on his face changed to narrow-eyed belligerence when he saw me. "You're not welcome here, Meikle."

I struggled to keep my voice pleasant. "I haven't come calling on you, Les. It's Larry I want to see. We have some business to discuss."

"What kind of business?"

"Personal."

I watched his knuckles whiten on the beer can and wondered if he was going to crush it in his fist like Popeye. I could imagine the fountain of amber liquid spraying all over Dorrie Taylor's pristine front hall. It would almost be worth it just to see Les make such a complete ass of himself.

He raised his chin. "You got a warrint or somethin'?"

"A warrant? Why would I need a warrant to talk to someone about a personal issue, Les?" I shook my head. "Where's Larry?"

"None o' your damn bizniss." Les moved to shut the door.

I stepped quickly over the threshold. Short of actually pushing me back out the door, Les couldn't move me. I remembered Mrs. Creighton's assessment of him and felt fairly sure that when push came to shove, Les wouldn't. I stared him down.

"You persist in thinking that nothing Larry does is any

of my 'damn bizniss', Les. And I can't tell you how happy I'd be never to set eyes on that . . ." I glanced at Dorrie Taylor's face "on him again. But if Larry is involved in poaching black bears—and I think he is—then it is very much my business. And when he leaves eviscerated rats on my doorstep, it stops being merely business and becomes a definite personal grievance. Now where is he?"

Les's sullen scowl was replaced by a look of malicious pleasure when I mentioned the rat. It was obviously not news to him; for all I knew, it had been his idea. Dorrie's pallid face went suddenly ashen. She swayed where she stood, making soft gagging noises.

"Mrs. Taylor . . ." I moved forward to help her. Les sprang between us, grabbing his daughter's arm.

"Get the hell out of my house, Meikle! And don't you come near me or mine again. You hear me? Keep away from my fam'ly!"

Dorrie Taylor simply looked at me with dull eyes, saying nothing.

There was nothing to be gained by staying. As I shut the door behind me, I could hear Les saying, "Come on, now Dorrie girl. Pull yerself t'gether."

I'm sure his daughter found great comfort in the words.

Personally, I felt like a simmering pot about to boil over. I'm not noted for the evenness of my temper, but I have always worked hard at keeping it under physical control, at least. Low-lifes like Larry and his pals bring out the worst in me. Les pissed me off, but only because I thought he was being stupid about protecting his grandson. We weren't talking about a ten-year old with minor behaviour problems, we were talking about a grown man who got his jollies trashing things. To my way of thinking, Larry Taylor was one sick puppy and the faster I could help him on his way to a vet, the better. All I had to do was find him.

His family would be no help. Protecting him had become second nature to them and I doubted they could have turned him in if they'd wanted to. I could go scouting around town for him. It was a pretty safe bet that he would be hanging out somewhere, drinking, probably in the inspired company of Curly and Moe. The idea of a public confrontation did not appeal. What was I supposed to do? Stride into the bar, gun drawn, and challenge the guy to a showdown? I had no authority for that. With the evidence I had, I couldn't even charge the guy with anything yet.

On the other hand, once I found him, it shouldn't be too difficult to keep him in view. If I was going to try my hand at private investigation, maybe I could practise a little first by devoting a couple of hours to sitting on Larry Taylor. It might yield results. There hadn't been a black bear incident for over a week. Larry must be running out of money. I cruised the most likely bars and finally ran the three stooges to ground at The Angler. That made sense. I should have started at the top.

For a Wednesday evening, the place was pretty crowded. The dartboard at the far end was getting a good work out and another little group was sitting glued to the TV. It looked like the Blue Jays and the Braves were playing. I spotted Larry and his pals at a small table in the corner. Judging by the number of empties, it had been a thirsty evening. Resisting the impulse to down a fast one myself, I went out again before Larry saw me. One bar fight a year is my limit.

I strolled around the parking lot looking for Larry's truck. Then I parked where I could keep an eye on it and get to the road easily myself when Larry left.

I doubted that anything worthwhile would happen that night. From the look of him, Larry was already several sheets to the wind and I didn't think even he would be stupid enough to go out bear hunting in that condition. Driving was another matter. A lot of people still don't subscribe to the no drinking and driving philosophy, especially good old boys like Larry.

It got pretty cold sitting there. I kept the tape player running so I could listen to Placido Domingo, but even his beautiful rendering of "Grenada" wasn't enough to warm me, and I had to turn the engine back on. Larry didn't come out until closing time. True to form, he and his buddies jumped into the truck and tore out of the parking lot like it was the start of the Indy 500. Luckily the streets were deserted and Larry managed to drop the Pearson boys off and get himself home without killing anyone on the way. I toyed with the idea of reporting him for driving under the influence but decided that the chances of anyone getting to him before he reached his own house were pretty slim. Judging by the record to date, even if the cops did grab him, he'd probably only end up with a slap on the wrist. I wanted much more for Larry than that.

I got out of my car and followed Larry to the door. My long, cold wait outside the bar had cooled my initial hot reaction to finding the dead rat on my doorstep, but some sixth sense prompted me to take a closer look.

Dorrie Taylor was still up when her son got home. The top half of the back door leading to her kitchen was glass and, as I approached the house, I could see Dorrie taking a small saucepan off the stove. Probably milk, I thought. With something in it to help her sleep. Dorrie jumped when Larry slammed the door. The milk spilled, scalding her hand. Her face crumpled in pain and as she moved to the sink in search of cold water for the burn, she let the pan drop to the floor. Some of the milk splashed over Larry's boots.

Larry was a mean drunk.

He turned on Dorrie, his face and voice tight with outrage. I saw him raise his right hand and slap his mother hard across the face. Dorrie rocked with the blow and stood, head bowed, not looking at her son, not moving to wipe away the blood that trickled from the side of her mouth.

I've been there. I remember the first time Nicholas hit me. I can still feel the stunning force of the blow against my cheekbone. I remember the moment of bewildered incomprehension and my total lack of response. Nicholas had been immediately contrite, horrified at himself, apologetic. "I'm sorry" is a phrase I never want to hear again. I tried to believe it. I tried to persuade myself that the incident was an aberration. Of course it wasn't. And since I'm relatively strong-minded, the second time it happened, outrage followed hard on the heels of surprise, and I fought back. I ended up with a broken arm, but left my marriage with my pride intact. Pride is the most valuable thing I possess; Dorrie Taylor desperately needed some. Without it, she'd never muster the strength to fight back.

In the next second, I was through the door and across the kitchen, jumping at Larry's back and hauling on the arm he had raised for another slap. He was much heavier than I and more used to brawling, but he was half-stupid with drink and that slowed him. I got my foot round behind him, and his own unbalanced weight propelled him backward over it, so that he tripped and fell sprawling onto the floor. As he fell, I gave his arm a quick shove that sent his hand flailing, for just a fraction of a second, onto the hot element of the stove. Larry screamed in pain, and scrabbled away from me, clutching his burned fingers.

There was a sound in the doorway behind me and I whirled to see Les standing there, hair tousled, pyjamas rumpled, gun in hand. I had an instant, sick understanding of a cop's reluctance to get involved in domestic violence. I imagined it would only take one wrong word from me to prompt Les to pull the trigger. I kept my mouth shut.

My stomach churned with a sickening combination of fear and something it took me a minute to identify as contempt—contempt for a man who would beat a woman, and for the woman who would let him.

It was Dorrie Taylor who finally broke the silence.

"Put the gun away, Dad," she said.

Les stared at her in surprise. "What're you talking about, girl? This bush cop," he fairly spat out the words, "has been assaultin' yer son. And I got a right to defend my fam'ly."

Dorrie's head came up and she gave her father a look with something new in it that made him take a step back. His hand relaxed a little on the trigger and I felt my breath go out in a rush. I hadn't realized that I had been holding it.

In measured tones, Dorrie said, "My son has just been assaulting me. Ms. Meikle stopped him." She added, "You should have stopped him, Dad. Years ago. We both should have."

The worm, I thought, was finally turning.

Dorrie moved her steady gaze to me. "You'd better go now." Her voice was low, but firm.

"Mrs. Taylor . . ." I faltered, searching for the right words to say, trying to excuse my interference in her family drama. Her expression told me not to bother. She had seen for herself the pleasure, however fleeting, it had given me to hurt Larry, and the disdain I had felt for her. That I was coldly ashamed of it now proved nothing.

As I went out the door, I glanced back at Larry, still huddled on the floor. The look on his face made it certain that if he, not Les, had been holding the gun, I would have been carried out of that house in a body bag.

CHAPTER **SEVENTEEN**

My appointment with Laura offered a convenient excuse to get out of town for a few days. The ugliness of the scene at the Taylors's had unsettled me more than I liked to admit. I hoped distance might give me some perspective on my own behaviour.

The little plane flew in low over Toronto harbour and landed on the tarmac at the Island airport. I had hitched a ride down with Warren Cunningham, owner of Geddes Air Charters. Warren did a lot of bush flying, and that day he was headed to Toronto to pick up a moose hunting party.

As we circled the airport, I could see heavy traffic moving along the major arteries feeding the city. Traffic in Toronto is always heavy; it doesn't seem to matter what time of day or night. Someone once wrote a popular song about a city that never sleeps. I think it was New York, but it could just as easily have been Toronto. All big cities tend to look alike to me, and they all inspire claustrophobia. Still, from the air, this one was pretty impressive. Warren pointed a stubby finger at the massive buildings that littered the waterfront. The Royal Bank Tower gleamed in the sunlight like a gold bar balanced on the edge of the lake.

"What is it about a scene like that—a cluster of skyscrapers in the distance—that makes you feel . . . what?—romantic? . . . excited?"

"Promise," I said.

"Promise?" Warren snorted. "What the hell of?"

"Of everything," I said. "From a distance they promise everything, anything, whatever you're after. They look clean and permanent. Like concrete castles in the air. It's not 'til you get up close that you notice all the shit dumped around the foundations."

I had tried to keep the disillusion out of my voice, but without much success.

Warren shot me a look. "So what are you saying Charlie, it's not real, the way they look from a distance?"

"No, I guess it's real enough. But so is the shit. And if you wander around on the ground looking up all the time, sooner or later you're bound to step in it."

Warren grinned. "Into each life some shit must fall?" I laughed, and let the tension ease from my shoulders.

On my way through the little terminal building, I passed a couple of middle-aged men who had traded in banker's grey for hunter green and were off for a wifeless weekend in the wilds. They looked soft around the middle, and stretched too tight around the eyes and mouth. One of them was pulling at his lower lip in a kind of nervous reflex. My bet was they'd spend more time quaffing beer and swapping tales than tracking down wildlife, but who cared? At home they probably analyzed profit and loss statements for fun.

I took the ferry across to downtown, standing on the open deck with the wind whipping my face and scavenging gulls circling and screeching around the boat. Over by the Royal Canadian Yacht Club, a cluster of sailboats was rounding a mark. As each boat cleared it, someone popped the kite and a brilliant-hued spinnaker billowed out, spilling colour the length of the downwind leg.

We docked with a minimum of fuss and I shouldered my bag, ready to do battle with the crowds. I debated taking a cab as Laura had suggested, but opted in favour of walking up to my hotel. I had a reservation at the Chestnut Park, right behind City Hall.

I got lost when I ducked into the train station looking for a coffee shop. One wrong turn and I was hustled into an endless underground labyrinth, propelled by a stream of people all walking purposefully forward with expressionless faces. Eventually, I managed to escape by squeezing onto an escalator going up, I hoped, toward light and air. A revolving door finally disgorged me onto the street.

Noise assaulted me from every direction. The city is a constant roar of traffic, construction equipment, and voices, some of which, presumably, are human.

It was only about a mile and a half from ferry dock to hotel lobby, but I was exhausted by the time I arrived. Luckily, the desk clerk didn't mind early check-ins. I ordered coffee from room service and took a revitalizing shower. Then I called Laura.

"You found the hotel all right?"

"Oh, sure, I brought my compass. Want to point me in the direction of your office?"

"I have a client coming in at two—shouldn't take too long, and I've kept the rest of the afternoon clear. How about three o'clock?"

I glanced at my watch. Three o'clock left me a couple of hours to kill. I didn't relish the idea of fighting off the hordes on the street again, so I took the shortest route to the World's Largest Bookstore and browsed contentedly until my stomach told me it was time to move on. I ate roast beef on a kaiser at a stand-up deli bar whose window overlooked the action on Yonge Street.

A mass of humanity seethed up and down the sidewalks. Kids who should have been in school hung out on the corners, wearing mismatched outfits so studiedly similar they could have been uniforms. Street vendors offered souvenir junk and printed T-shirts for sale at bargain prices. Two guys in suits and purple hair handed out flyers that promised eternal salvation.

A woman of indeterminate age shuffled by my window dragging a wire cart loaded with an untidy assortment of stuff that probably represented the sum total of her worldly possessions. She was a large woman, constructed in circles like the Michelin man, with a body lumpy from overweight or maybe just from all the layers of clothing she wore.

Slim, well-dressed secretaries who, judging by the bags they carried, had spent the lunch hour shopping, scurried back to their offices on high heels; the executives in tasselled loafers walked more slowly, with the carefully measured tread of success.

I finished my sandwich, made a quick tour of the Eaton Centre, and followed Laura's directions to her office, still managing to arrive fifteen minutes early. Her secretary was just getting ready to leave.

"Early closing today," the young woman told me with a grin. "If it's you I have to thank, then thanks."

The nameplate on her desk read Tracy Semple, and she had the fresh, eager look of one not long out of school.

Her hair was rather aggressively blonde, but the colour suited her fair skin and did nothing to detract from her obvious intelligence. Tucking a stack of mail under her arm, Tracy left me with a smile and a wave.

Apparently the coffee pot had been unplugged once Laura's two o'clock client had been satisfied, but on my way into the building I had noticed a take-out off the lobby. I filled in the time refortifying myself and at three went back upstairs.

Laura's office echoed the casual elegance of her clothes. Apart from a bank of sturdy file cabinets against the near wall, all the furniture in the room was antique. Beautifully restored and highly polished, it gleamed under recessed lighting and the glow of a banker's lamp. The window blinds were open, giving a fine view of nothing in particular. Across a narrow space was the sullen back of a red brick building, and below, delivery vans blocked the narrow street. Laura seemed very much at home and very much in charge as she ushered me to a comfortable leather chair facing her desk.

"Nice office."

"Thanks."

"My view is better."

"Whose isn't? The only thing that could beat this is a factory wall."

"Doesn't it make you feel claustrophobic?"

"What, my office?"

"No, the city."

She shrugged. "I'm comfortable here." Her tone became businesslike. "I did manage to track down the owner of the Windrush Mine. As you already know, the mine is controlled by a holding company. That company owns and operates a number of businesses including, among other things, a small trucking firm and an investment company. It also has ties to an organization called Save Our Planet. Ever heard of it?"

I gave a snort of disgust.

Laura smiled. "I'll interpret that as a yes. Anyway, the long and the short of it is, that a fellow called T. David Beare owns the controlling interest in all of the above. Apparently he inherited everything except Save Our Planet from his daddy. That one is a relatively new enterprise. Unfortunately, Mr. Beare doesn't seem to have inherited any kind of business acumen to go along with it all. None of his enterprises is financially successful. The Windrush is closed down, the trucking company has been losing money hand over fist for the last couple of years, and the investment company doesn't seem to have a lot to invest. Save Our Planet is doing fine, donations are up all the time, but, since it's a charitable organization, you wouldn't expect any vast profits to be rolling in from that."

I frowned. "Does T. David Beare have an office?"

"He does," Laura nodded, "but he's a hard man to see. I tried to get an appointment with him for you, but his secretary was extremely vague about his whereabouts. She said if I gave her specifics, she could 'direct me to the appropriate source of information'. That's how she talks—very pleasant, friendly manner, but stonewalling you all the same. I wasn't sure how far you wanted me to push it." She paused. "Since you haven't told me yet what this is all about . . ."

Her tone was pointed. I ignored it.

"What about the acting heads of all these companies? Could I talk to them, do you think?"

Laura shrugged. "I would imagine so. But what exactly are you hoping to find out?"

It was the same question Neil Ewing had asked at the mine. What are you looking for? My answer then had been that I wasn't sure. My answer now was the criminal idiot who is storing toxic garbage in a disused mine shaft.

The question of using old mines for just this purpose has been a hot item on the environmental discussion table for years, but so far no one in the provincial or the federal governments is empowered to approve it. And even if they were, the dumpsite certainly would not be left unmonitored.

Clearly, this was a private enterprise, and one that was going seriously wrong.

CHAPTER **EIGHTEEN**

There was no way Laura was going to let me off the hook. We'd made a deal. She'd lived up to her end; the determination in her face told me it was time to live up to mine.

"It's kind of a long story," I warned.

Laura merely settled back more comfortably in her chair. She listened attentively, gently chewing on her lower lip, as I laid out fact and theory as coherently as I could.

She was impatient over the technical details of the chemical waste and its effect on the life of Finger Lake.

She was shocked over the bear poaching scenario, repulsed by my description of Larry, outraged at his abuse of his mother. There were tears in her eyes when I told her about Irene Creighton's dog.

She said nothing throughout my long recitation, but her face was easy to read. I hoped, for her sake, that she never played poker. By the time I finished, her mobile features were frozen into an expression of pain and acceptance. Her conclusions about Jim Griffith's death were clearly the same as mine.

Outside, the steady hum of traffic was rudely interrupted by a blare of horns. Some poor bugger on his way home had stalled at an intersection. Twenty-five irate motorists were blasting away in unison to help him restart his engine. Along the street, lights blinked on and neon signs buzzed against the darkening sky. I got up from my chair to stretch muscles stiffened from sitting too long in one position.

Laura cleared her throat. "What are we going to do?"

"We?"

"I loved him, Charlie." Her tone implied that everything that needed to be had been said. And in a way, I suppose it had. What did it matter if she was motivated by guilt or debt or loneliness? Who wasn't? In the end, for both of us, it all came down to love.

"Okay. I think our first step should be to talk to whoever is in charge at that trucking company—what's it called?

Laura shuffled some papers. "Um . . . Burden Transport. Operates a fleet of smaller trucks and vans. Their motto is 'Let us carry your load'." She smiled. "Cute logo: an army of ants on roller skates. Their head office is here in Toronto, the west end." She glanced at the clock on her desk. "They're probably closed now, though. On Fridays a lot of businesses close down early."

Nonetheless, she picked up the phone and dialled the number listed on the page in front of her. A minute later, she made a face at the receiver and hung up. "No answer. Just a recording, saying their offices are closed until seven AM Monday and giving an emergency number to call if you have a problem with a current shipment."

"I guess we'll have to leave them 'til Monday then. What about SOP?"

"What?"

"SOP. The Save Our Planet people. They might be open at least part of the day Saturday. I wouldn't think saving the world could be limited to five days a week."

Laura raised an eyebrow at the acid in my voice. "What have you got against—what did you call them—SOP? I'd have thought you'd support any group that tries to help save the environment."

I shook my head. "The problem with these activist groups is that they tend to go off half-cocked. They grab hold of a single issue, or worse, part of an issue, and then pull off some grandstanding stunt for the media that really only accomplishes one thing and that's the promotion of the group itself."

"But you can't deny that SOP and others like them have done a lot to raise people's awareness of environmental issues," Laura argued. "Look how far we've come in the past ten years with recycling programs, for example, or wilderness preservation."

"Oh, yeah, I know, everybody's got a blue box. And that's great, don't get me wrong. I think it's terrific that people are more aware of what they're throwing away. The problem is, a lot of people have the idea that their responsibility begins and ends there—that if they use their little blue box and buy an acre of rainforest, they've done their bit for the environment. They don't seem to understand, and organizations like SOP don't try to help them understand, that that's all it is. A bit. A drop in the bucket. One tiny piece of the puzzle. What we need to do is look at the whole puzzle, try to understand how all the little pieces fit together. To see that when you take one piece out, or damage it, all the pieces around it are affected."

Laura looked a little dazed by my outburst, but once

I'm up on my soapbox it takes more than a blank expression to stop me.

"It's all very well to raise a banner and go marching off to stop the slaughter of seal pups. They're cute and furry and they make it easy to get public support on your side while you do your thing. But don't forget while you're doing it, to take into account the effect that an increased seal population will have on fish stocks. And what effect decreased fish stocks will have on other aquatic life.

"SOP targets issues that give it the most popular support. It leaves people with the impression that the environment will be safe from harm if only that particular evil is eliminated. It's misleading as hell."

I stopped, a little embarrassed by my own vehemence.

Laura didn't want to let it go. "So you think the three Rs of the nineties are just cute little buzzwords?"

"Not at all. But I think the fourth R is the most important one. Responsibility."

"You mean limiting the use of certain chemicals, fining the transgressor, stuff like that?"

I shook my head. "I mean Joe Average taking responsibility on a day-to-day basis. Deciding it's not that vital if his letterhead is printed on brown paper rather than bleached. Realizing that if he doesn't buy mahogany, there's no need to cut down a rainforest to supply it. It's easy enough to point the finger and say if only the big corporation cleans up its act how much better the world will be. Much harder to point the finger at yourself. I think that not wanting to know where you fit in, not being willing to accept individual responsibility for your place, is the snare that is going to bring us all down."

I got up and moved to the window, action halting the flow of my own words. It was fully dark out now. Smoked glass oblongs stared blankly at me from the building across the street; lights shone only from the few offices where dedicated workaholics still toiled. My throat felt dry and my stomach empty. It seemed a long time since the sandwich at the deli bar.

I smiled apologetically at Laura. "I think I'll climb down off my soapbox now. Where can we get some dinner?"

She tidied the papers on her desk and replaced a couple of heavy volumes on the bookshelf behind her. "What are you in the mood for? French, Italian, Chinese, East Indian? We have it all."

I shrugged. "It's up to you. I eat anything that isn't moving. Except Brussels sprouts."

She laughed. "Well, that certainly narrows the field. Let's see what we can find."

She finally opted for an Italian restaurant located in an old warehouse, a cavernous high-ceilinged room whose functional atmosphere had been replaced by warm lighting and cosy groupings of tables. Oak beams and random scatterings of greenery gave the illusion of privacy. A solicitous hostess ushered us to upholstered chairs at a table neatly laid with linen and pewter. Smiling, she left us with menus. A waiter scurried over to fill our water glasses and deposit a basket of crusty bread along with a shallow dish of oil.

"It's for dipping the bread in," Laura said, amused at my confusion. "Instead of butter. That's extra virgin olive oil, very low in cholesterol."

"I see. Butter is a no-no? No more garlic bread?"

"You got it."

"Mm. Judgement reserved." Actually, it was very good, as was the rest of the meal. We chatted through most of it about nothing in particular, shelving for the moment any discussion of Jim Griffith or the problems at Finger Lake.

"What's it like," Laura wanted to know, "living in a place like Geddes Lake? I mean, what is there to do there when you're not working?"

"Same things people do anywhere. Read, listen to music, play sports, join clubs."

"But," she frowned, "don't you feel sort of cut off up there?"

"Cut off from what? Overcrowding? Traffic?"

"Who'd miss those? No, I meant what about theatre and so on?"

I tried to look affronted. "We do have the Geddes Lake Little Theatre Company. They put on a show a few times a year. It's not Stratford, but it's not bad stuff."

I didn't tell her that for the first time, I had accepted a performing role in their upcoming production of *My Fair Lady*. Usually I shun the footlights in favour of working behind the scenes, but this year the company had decided to forgo its standard dramatic offering and produce a musical. The high school orchestra, which had scored a first at the Kiwanis festival, was providing the backup and I couldn't resist the chance to dress up and sing on stage. My voice wasn't good enough to win the lead, but I was happy enough as Professor Higgins's housekeeper.

The waiter brought refills for our coffee and at the same time unobtrusively placed the bill in the middle of the table. Laura reached for it. "I'll get it. I can expense it."

While we waited at the coat check to redeem our tickets, a striking couple made an entrance and posed by the reception desk. The woman had a long spill of blonde hair and lots of teeth; her escort was carefully brushed and styled, a vicuna coat slung carelessly over one shoulder. They spoke in the bright, artificial tones of the self-consciously cool, carrying on a conversation of nuances that seemed to leave the most important part of every sentence unexpressed.

Laura's eyes widened in dismay when she spotted Vicuna Coat. He recognized her in the same instant.

"Laura!" he cried dramatically, taking both her hands in his. "What a surprise running in to you here! Haven't seen you for ages. I've been meaning to call . . ."

"Have you?" Laura's voice was tight and she turned her head to avoid his kiss. "Are you ready to go, Charlie?"

Vicuna Coat swung his glance over me in swift, dismissive appraisal. Just so had Nicholas graded the women in a room. Once, it had been desperately important to me to be noticed by a dazzler such as this one. Now, I judged him as critically, and dismissed him as easily, as he did me.

I saw the blonde shift restlessly from one foot to the other, her gaiety replaced by petulance. Introductions were obviously not in order.

"Don't let us keep you from your dinner," I said pleasantly. "I highly recommend the cuisine. The virgin olive oil is particularly good."

The blonde gave me a blank look, but Vicuna Coat

actually curled his lip at me as they swept away to their table. I glanced at Laura. She was biting her lip hard. I couldn't tell if she was holding back a laugh or tears.

"Who was that?"

She pretended amazement. "You mean you didn't recognize him? What a blow to his ego that'll be. That was the great Mark Dyment, star of the ever-popular TV series *Dirty Business*."

I thought for a minute. "Does he play the part of the big wheel in mergers and acquisitions?"

"That's him."

"The one who targets a new company and a new babe every week?"

"You got it."

The residual bitterness in her tone made it clear that so had she. Personally, I didn't think she was out much.

"What's the game plan for tomorrow?" she asked as we went down the steps to the street.

"SOP's offices, I think."

"Okay. How about I pick you up at your hotel around ten?"

"Ten's fine," I said. "I'll meet you in the lobby."

CHAPTER **NINETEEN**

Save Our Planet was on the second floor of a three-story walk-up. The best that could be said for the building was that the rent was probably cheap. Laura and I went up dimly lit stairs, past the office of a consultant (in what, was not specified), and knocked on the door that had Save Our Planet spelled out in green over a blue and grey painted Earth. A neatly printed sign, also in green, told us to "Please enter."

Inside, an earnest-looking young woman, maybe nineteen years old, smiled up at us from behind a desk littered with pamphlets and flyers. I didn't see a nameplate, which wasn't surprising. The office was probably staffed by a string of volunteers. This one had dark, curly hair loosely caught back in a clip, and a dedicated expression. Huge tortoiseshell glasses sat squarely on the end of her nose. She paused in her typing to ask, "Can I help you?"

I returned her smile. "I'm trying to get in touch with Mr. Beare."

She blinked. "I beg your pardon?"

"Mr. Beare. T. David Beare. I understand he's connected with Save Our Planet."

The girl frowned. "I'm afraid I . . ."

The buzzer on her desk sounded, startling her into silence. The door to our left opened to reveal a pallid, middle-aged man of average height, whose skin was pitted by the scars of old acne, and whose black ponytail was liberally sprinkled with grey. He wore jeans and scruffy boots, a checked shirt and, incredibly, a fringed leather vest. I hadn't seen one of those in years. It made him look like a time-warp hippie. I half expected to see him raise two fingers in salute and say, "Peace, brother."

But he merely surveyed us, unmoving, from the doorway and when he did speak, it was to reiterate the girl's question. "Can I help you?"

I knew that boom-box voice. This must be the great Frank Dennison himself. I'd seen his face and heard his voice a thousand times. He looked bigger on TV, more significant. Real life diminished him.

"Mr. Dennison," I said, stepping forward to shake hands. He returned the gesture as briefly as possible. "Charlie Meikle. I'm a conservation officer, from Geddes Lake. And this is Laura Rhodes."

"Also a conservation officer?"

"No," Laura said. "A lawyer."

Dennison's eyebrows rose fractionally.

I said, "I understand a gentleman by the name of Beare is fairly active behind the scenes of Save Our Planet and I was hoping you or someone in your organization could help me get in touch with him."

"Why?" There was suspicion in Dennison's tone, and a hint of something else. The earnest young woman abruptly resumed her typing.

I picked my words carefully, trying to disarm. "Mr. Beare has several other business interests. I want to speak with him in connection with one of those not directly related to Save Our Planet."

"Which interest?"

I felt Laura stiffen at the rudeness of his tone, but her own voice was even as she replied, "A mine in northern Ontario. Do you know where we could contact Mr. Beare?"

"He has an office."

"Yes," said Laura, dryly. "And a secretary."

Dennison smiled brief acknowledgement of that woman's skill as a blocker. He studied us through hooded eyes for another minute, then jerked his head toward his office.

"Hold my calls," he told the typist.

I didn't see a jammed switchboard as one of SOP's major problems, but Dennison was that kind of guy, the type who would always be on the phone long-distance when you showed up for an appointment.

The three of us settled in an office furnished by garage sale. Dennison indicated a coffee pot flanked by china mugs, all bearing the SOP logo. No polystyrene here. Laura declined the offer, but I accepted and barely managed not to gag as the first mouthful went down. It was decaf.

"So," said Dennison. "What's all this about some mine?"

I let Laura field that one in polite legalese that effectively said, none of your business. Dennison didn't like it. While the two of them danced around the question, I studied the room. It was decorated in slogans and eco-campaign posters. Mounted on one wall was a huge corkboard covered in newspaper clippings interspersed with a few photographs. One photograph in particular caught my eye and I got up for a closer look.

It was a wide-angle shot of Dennison standing beside a small, twin-engine plane. In the background, to his left in the picture, the head frame of a mine was just visible over the tops of the trees. I squinted at it to bring it into better focus. As I leaned forward, I became aware that Laura and Frank Dennison were both looking at me expectantly. From their expressions, I gathered that they were waiting for me to answer a question I hadn't heard.

"I'm sorry. What did you say?"

It was Dennison who answered. "I was just telling Ms. Rhodes here that we seem to be at an impasse. You do not wish to enlighten me as to your reasons for seeking out Mr. Beare and, frankly, without that information, I cannot see my way clear to giving you any assistance in locating him. The man is one of Save Our Planet's chief benefactors. I would be most unwilling to jeopardize our relationship by indiscriminately passing on information he may wish to keep private. In any case," he went on smugly, "I have no first-hand knowledge of any of Mr. Beare's other business involvements."

I felt my teeth clench. Naively, I had assumed that the clotted jargon I was used to hearing from him was for media consumption only. Unfortunately, it seemed to be his usual conversational style.

"Nice plane," I said, nodding at the photograph. "You fly it yourself?"

"Yes, I do, as a matter of fact." He sounded self-congratulatory.

"Do you get up north often?"

"Fairly." His tone became guarded.

"This scene looks kind of familiar." I gestured again.

"Isn't that the Windrush Mine there in the background?"

Dennison gave me a measuring look. "I believe it might be."

"What a coincidence! The Windrush is right in my own backyard." I gave him a winning smile. "I'm from Geddes Lake, did I say?"

"Yes."

"Ah. I guess it didn't ring a bell."

A vein in Dennison's left temple started to throb, drawing attention to his bright little blueberry eyes. They stared at me, unwavering.

"I have travelled to a great many different locales in my capacity as Chief Environmental Investigator of Save Our Planet," he said haughtily. "I could hardly be expected to remember each and every one of them. But now that you mention it, yes, I was up in the Geddes Lake area once or twice. By personal invitation." His smile lasted a microsecond.

"Whose?"

"I beg your pardon?"

"I said 'whose'? Whose invitation?"

Dennison's voice was icy. "I really cannot see that that is any of your business."

"Maybe not," I said easily. "I only asked because I know a lot of the folks in and around the area. Thought we might have some common acquaintance . . ."

Dennison was silent for a minute. His gaze flicked from me to Laura and back to me again while he made up his mind what to tell us. I wondered how close to the truth his response would be.

He stood up to refill his coffee cup. "Well, you've got

me." He had adopted the boom-box voice again, brimming with sincerity and good intentions. "As it happens, I flew up to Geddes Lake at the invitation of Mr. Beare. He wanted me to look over a mine site he owned. I believe Windrush was the name of it."

He beamed at me as if I were a successful game show contestant. When I didn't react, he went on, "The mine was apparently shut down some years ago. Mr. Beare solicited my opinion on the viability of turning the property to other uses. He seeks in some small measure to compensate for the inevitable environmental damage resulting from his mining operation. As you may be aware, there is a movement afoot, spearheaded I might add, by Save Our Planet, to redeem land once thought irretrievably lost." Dennison picked up a sheaf of printed flyers and waved them at me. "We have helped to establish replanting campaigns in several locations and it is one of our ongoing concerns to research other possible uses for such sites. Mr. Beare is an active participant in our program."

Dennison's florid rhetoric left me speechless, as no doubt it was meant to. Laura, however, was made of sterner stuff when it came to cutting through evasive wordplay.

"That's very interesting, Mr. Dennison. What are the specifics of the program you recommended for the Windrush Mine? Replanting, or . . . other uses?"

"That is a confidential matter for the directors of the Windrush Mine."

"Confidential?"

"Yes."

"Why? What's so secret about it?"

"There is nothing secret about it, Ms. Rhodes." Dennison was losing patience. "It is simply none of our business. And I cannot see that it is any of yours."

"Gee," I said, "I thought you guys made everything your business. Especially when you've been called in specially to do just that. Aren't you curious about the outcome of your visit? Don't you want to know what Mr. Beare decided to do with his empty mine site?"

I had been moving steadily closer as I spoke, so that by the time I finished I was leaning over the desk, my face just a few inches from Frank Dennison's. He leaned further back in his chair to get out of range.

"Exactly what point are you trying to make, Ms. Meikle?"

"I'm surprised, that's all. Surprised that you don't seem to have done any follow up at all on the situation at the Windrush. Or maybe you have. Maybe you already know that your good friend and supporter of environmental causes T. David Beare is using the place as a storage site for toxic chemicals."

Dennison recoiled as though struck.

"That's right, Frank. He's been piling up drums full of liquid junk in the shaft. The trouble is, they've been leaking, and for more than just a little while. They've been leaching into the aquifer and percolating through the rocks and you can probably guess the kind of damage they've been doing to the lake they're seeping down into."

Dennison's face was pale. He seemed to be concentrating very hard on the fringes of his vest. I noticed he wore a gold pin fairly high on the right side of it, an oblong tie tack with an intricate design engraved on it that might have been a bird in flight. It looked hand-made, not mass-produced.

Dennison made no move to break the heavy silence.

Finally I asked, "Are you going to tell me where I can find Mr. Beare?"

Dennison shook his head.

I pressed. "You know his dumping operation will be shut down. The cleanup at the site has already been started. The police are going to be looking for the man."

Dennison said nothing.

I looked at Laura. For once, her expression was unreadable. With a snort of disgust, I headed for the door.

"Have a nice day, Frank."

CHAPTER **TWENTY**

As soon as we were safely out of earshot, Laura exploded. "He knows all about it!"

We were standing in the tiny foyer of the Save Our Planet building. Pale sunlight filtered through narrow windows onto faded grey walls, where hand-lettered signs published the names of the tenants. A persistent beeping announced that a delivery truck outside was backing up the lane beside the building.

"Of course he knows," I said. "He's probably known all along. But Dennison's caught between the proverbial rock and a hard place. Here's a guy whose whole reason for being is to expose environmental abuses, but who's totally dependent on financial handouts to do it. Now it turns out his biggest contributor is one of the biggest abusers. What'd you expect him to do? Blow the whistle?"

"Yes!"

"No way. Look at it from his point of view. If he turns Beare in, he loses his major source of funding. He's probably persuaded himself that making an issue out of this one particular incident isn't worth the risk of losing his whole operation."

Laura rounded on me in a fury. "Risk? What risk? Dennison could easily have gone to the papers or the TV and exposed the dumping at the Windrush. It would have won him a ton of popular support. In time he could have found other financial backers—there are plenty of people around looking for tax deductions." She was shaking. "He just didn't have the guts to stand up to T. David Beare. So Finger Lake was contaminated and Jim Griffith found out about it. And Jim did have the guts for confrontation, only he didn't have any media hype to protect him. For God's sake, Charlie, don't you see? Because Frank Dennison wimped out, Jim Griffith died!"

"We don't know that for sure," I said gently.

"Don't we? You're the one who suggested murder in the first place, Charlie, remember? You pointed out to me all the reasons for not believing Jim's death was accidental. You're the one who came up with a motive. Why are you backpedalling now? You know as well as I do that that man upstairs cost Jim Griffith his life!"

I hadn't expected to touch a nerve with Frank Dennison. I'd only been looking for a conduit to Beare, but Dennison's knowledge of the situation at the Windrush opened up a whole new set of possibilities. I was thinking about the newspaper clipping I had found among Jim's things. Had Jim actually contacted Dennison before calling me? Had he planned to go public about the dumping at the Windrush? I wouldn't have thought it was Jim's style, but with the health of his beloved lake at stake, he may have seen it as a necessary evil. Someone else had seen it as a personal threat. Frank Dennison? Or David Beare?

Back in the car Laura said, "What's next? Do we call in the police?"

"And say what? That there's illegal dumping going on? Paul Ewing's already taken care of all that. The Ministry of Environment wants to keep things relatively quiet while they assess the possibilities for cleanup. Criminal charges will be laid under the Environmental Protection Act as soon as the police catch up with Beare. Unfortunately, we still don't have any hard evidence linking any of this to Jim Griffith's death. So far we can't even locate David Beare."

"But surely, the police . . ."

"Of course. The OPP will be able to track him down. And they'll figure out exactly who's to blame for what as far as the toxic waste goes. What about Jim though? We think that someone murdered him, but all we have right now is theory and conjecture. I'm not sure that's enough to convince the police to start a murder investigation."

"So what do we do? We can't just let it go."

"No," I agreed, "we can't do that. We'll have to keep poking around until we turn up something concrete. Our little interview with Dennison only muddied the waters. I'd envisioned a straight line between Beare, the Windrush and Jim. Now I'm not so sure."

"Do you think Dennison had something to do with Jim's death?"

I shook my head slowly. "Not directly. Unless he's worked out a way of being in two places at once."

"What do you mean?"

"I was listening to an interview with Frank Dennison on *Talk It Out* just a few minutes before I found Jim. Those shows are always done live at the studio in Toronto. So there's no way Dennison could have been at Finger Lake that day."

A guy in a red Buick tooted an impatient horn at us. I glanced at my watch. We had been sitting in the car for fifteen minutes. With parking spaces at a premium, I couldn't blame the guy for being peeved. He'd probably driven around the block half a dozen times waiting for us to leave. Laura started the car. She gave the red Buick an embarrassed wave, and he gave her a look that said, "Women."

I said, "It looks like a dead end for today. T. David Beare isn't listed in the phone book, so we can't mount an assault on his home. Burden Transport is closed, so we have to wait 'til Monday to see what we can find out there. I don't know about you, but I could use a pick me up. Any good coffee shops around?"

"You're addicted," she accused.

"Absolutely."

"Well, you're in luck. Because I happen to know of a terrific European pastry shop not too far from here."

"Pastry? Don't tell me . . ."

She nodded ruefully. "Yep. Whipped cream. My secret sin."

"Your secret's safe with me."

Afternoon dwindled to evening. We dined on gourmet pizza, which is something of an oxymoron and not nearly as satisfying as pepperoni. Laura invited me back to her place for coffee.

After the warmth of her office, I was surprised by the starkness of her home. There were no polished antiques here. The apartment was furnished with boxy pieces of blonde wood upholstered in dark blue fabric unrelieved by any pattern. Several oil paintings, all angles and harsh lines, hung from the walls. Little plaques on the edge of the frames marked them as gallery rentals. There were no pillows, no plants, no warm pools of light to soften the rigidity of the arrangement.

"This is very . . . functional looking," I said.

"You don't like it."

I shrugged.

"You don't. That's all right, I'm not sure I like it all that much myself anymore. It suited me fine when I first put it together, everything sort of clean and uncluttered looking."

"An apartment, not a home," I suggested. "What about all the antiques at your office?"

"Oh, those were Jim's. He insisted I take them when he retired."

Laura served good coffee in big ceramic mugs. Hers was plain, mine, a cartoon of two bucks at the edge of the forest. One had a red bulls-eye in the middle of his chest. His buddy was saying, "Bummer of a birthmark, Hal."

"Mark gave it to me," Laura explained. "I've got a birthmark here on my neck. It's always embarrassed me. Mark thought I should lighten up about it. The mug was his idea of joke therapy."

"Sensitive guy."

The corners of her mouth twitched, whether in agreement or annoyance, I couldn't tell.

"You were married, right?"

I nodded. "Briefly."

"What happened?"

"Whoa, I need something a lot stronger than coffee before I talk about Nicholas."

While she poured it, I made a trip to the john that took me through Laura's bedroom. An ancient stuffed bear regarded me solemnly from a wicker chair by the door and I noticed a dog-eared copy of *The Watch that Ends the Night* on top of a low bookshelf crammed with an eclectic assortment of reading material. The bureau was littered with framed photographs, mostly of a little girl growing up between handsome, aristocratic looking parents, and one of Laura alone, looking solemn in her graduation gown, her arms full of roses. There were two pictures of Jim, one that I remembered taking at the first annual Finger Lake Fishing Derby. Jim was showing off the prize catch of the day. The second picture was a close-up. Jim was smiling directly into the camera with a look that told me Laura had been behind it.

It was a room full of memories. The rest of the apartment was for show; this room was for living in. Maybe Laura and I had more in common than I'd thought.

The wine bottle was almost empty. We had abandoned coffee in favour of Chablis and were ensconced at opposite ends of the couch, with our feet crossing in the middle, like teenagers. Conversation had progressed to a down and dirty discussion of the things that really matter.

"But don't you miss the regular sex? " Laura demanded. She drained the bottle and held it to her eye, as though suspecting a final drop of holding out on her. "That's the thing I hate most about being single. " She lowered the bottle and tried to balance it on her kneecap. "One night stands are the pits. On the other hand, 'enduring relationships' are mighty hard to come by. No pun intended."

In a confidential tone, I said, "Chocolate chip cookies."
"What?"

"I said, 'chocolate chip cookies.' They are the real secret of life."

Laura regarded me gravely. "You figure?"

"Absolutely. A friend of mine asked me once which I'd rather have, sex or a warm chocolate chip cookie. And I said, a chocolate chip cookie."

"Why?"

"'Cause I can bake the cookies myself."

I took a taxi back to my hotel around eleven. The cabbie drove with the windows open, and the night air was crisp enough to dispel the haze inspired by the wine. I spent the rest of the night watching movies on Home Box Office. I don't sleep well out of my own environment and Toronto is definitely an alien land to me. Its sights and sounds make me edgy and besides, I don't get cable at home.

We met for brunch at the momentarily fashionable uptown restaurant that Laura insisted on, the kind of place where people "do" lunch, rather than eat it. The menu offered insubstantial sounding fare at ridiculous prices. A waiter rhapsodized over three dishes so original they were not yet listed and, out of desperation, I chose one of those. When it arrived, I eyed a meagre helping of eggs scrambled with kiwi and thought longingly of Dot's Blue Plate Special. On the other hand, the coffee was good and the pot bottomless.

Halfway through our meal, a flurry of activity at the door and a hurried rearranging of tables near the window heralded the arrival of the ubiquitous Mark Dyment, accompanied this morning by a coterie of adoring hangers-on. As he removed his coat (leather today),

Dyment scanned the room, smiling gracious recognition as several people waved. His roving glance passed our table, halted and came back. Across from me, Laura straightened in her chair and lifted her chin slightly in Dyment's direction. The high voltage smile became a little more fixed as he inclined his head, then turned away.

I stared at Laura. The colour had risen in her cheeks. She opened her mouth to speak, and then shut it again. We finished the meal in silence. Neither of us looked at Mark Dyment on our way out.

I wanted to say, "get over it," but I remembered my own sideways drift into a relationship that had become an obsession, and I bit my tongue. It galled me to think of the time I'd spent following Nicholas with puppy-like devotion and a sexual hunger that humiliated me now. I had let him do things to me that I had only read about in books, not realizing that it wasn't me he was making love to, but himself. I didn't know where Laura's fascination with Mark Dyment had led, but I was in no position to criticize.

"Why don't you say it?" Laura asked.

"Say what?"

"What you're thinking: that I'm a weak-minded fool."

I sighed. "Who hasn't been?"

Constraint faded with the dull light of an overcast afternoon. We wandered for an hour through the fallen leaves of High Park, beside a pond as grey and greasy as Kipling's Limpopo, and by the time we went our separate ways, I felt we'd taken a big step towards friendship. To celebrate, I treated myself to a thick, rare steak, and a bottle of wine in the hotel dining room.

CHAPTER **TWENTY-ONE**

I swung my rental car into a slot just inside the main gate at Burden Transport and followed the signs to the office. I was on my own today; Laura had a court date.

A shiny new Porsche slanted possessively across two reserved parking spaces. It was black with a burgundy interior and undoubtedly a statement. Someone at Burden must be doing well.

To my right, a black van with a logo of red ants on roller skates was pulling into the compound adjacent to the office. "Burden Transport. Let us carry your load" was stencilled above the toiling insects. As the gate swung open to admit the van, two large German shepherds padded over from the guardhouse for a sniff. One of the dogs suddenly raised his head in my direction and I took an involuntary step backwards. A similar scene at the Windrush Mine sprang vividly to mind. I looked at the black van appraisingly.

It would be no surprise if Burden Transport was part of the picture. The toxic waste stored at the Windrush had to be moved somehow and it only made sense that Beare would keep it in the family, so to speak. Whether anyone at Burden was directly involved was another question.

Inside the main building a matronly secretary with no-nonsense hair handed me a cup of steaming coffee, led me straight into the boss's office, and sat me down facing his desk. The office was a trophy hunter's dream. A moose head on my right traded looks with a morose assortment of smaller prizes on my left. I sat on the edge of my seat like a sixth-grader expecting a reprimand. The boss at Burden looked every bit as formidable as Mr. Purvis, but I thought even Carole might have trouble visualizing his brawn in shining armour.

He was swivelled sideways in his chair when I entered the room, pencilling information on a chart pinned to the wall. His hieroglyphics were unintelligible, but the chart looked like some kind of schedule planner, with headings marked size of truck, destination, and so on. Judging by the number of spaces already filled in, Burden was a busy outfit. I cleared my throat. He swivelled round fast, sticking out a beefy hand in an automatic gesture. "Matt Donnelly. What can I do for you?" His gravelly voice conjured visions of earthmovers and front-end loaders. I noticed he wore his watch on his right wrist. Either he was a lefty like me, or he wanted people to notice the gold Rolex.

I returned the handshake. "Charlie Meikle. I appreciate your time."

Donnelly did a small double take before his mouth tightened into a businesslike smile.

"I'm trying to locate a fellow named David Beare. I understand he has some connection to this company."

Donnelly's friendly expression closed in a little, but he answered pleasantly enough. "That's right. He owns it. But I run it for him. Anything you want to know about Burden, I'm the one to ask. Anything you want to know about Beare . . ." he shrugged. "I don't keep personal tabs on the guy. I meet with him once a month, here, to go over the accounts, discuss any problems. Why don't you try his office?"

"I have. They don't seem too willing to put me in touch with him."

"No? What do you want him for, anyway?" The tone was casual.

I weighed my answer, trying to decide if Donnelly was an innocent bystander or a very good blocker.

"Something personal."

"Oh. Well. Can't help you. Sorry." He sounded relieved. "Anything else?" His eyes were already straying back to the chart on the wall.

"I might be interested in renting a truck," I said. "Or maybe a van."

"Yeah?"

"Yeah. If I rented from Burden, what restrictions would apply? Would I have to use the truck within a certain area or anything?"

Donnelly shook his head. "Nope. 'Course, we'd want to have some idea of where you're taking it and when you plan to bring it back. Most people use our trucks for short hauling, local moves, that kind of thing. We have a few on long term leases. What'd you need the truck for?"

"Oh," I said vaguely, "I have some furniture and stuff I need to move up north."

"No problem. One way trip?"

"What do you mean?"

"You returning the truck here or looking to drop it off somewhere else?"

"Can I do that?"

"Sure. We have other yards. North, you said? Sudbury, Timmins, North Bay? Any of those close?"

"Timmins. Geddes Lake, actually, but I don't think you have a yard there." Was it my imagination or had Donnelly's eyes flickered at the mention of Geddes Lake?

"Timmins. Right. No problem. You pick the truck up here, load your stuff, drop it off in Timmins. Daily charge plus taxes and insurance. We need a driver's licence, permanent address, and a major credit card."

I nodded. "You ever check on what people move in your trucks?"

Donnelly grinned. "None of my business. We're not a hauling company. As long as they don't trash the vehicle, what people move is up to them."

"What if it's illegal?"

The grin faded. Donnelly hunched his shoulders. It made him look even bigger. "What're you getting at?"

Absurdly, I found myself tensing, bracing against potential attack. Despising the sudden attack of nerves, I said calmly, "I was merely wondering what kind of control, if any, you have over the cargo that gets moved around in your trucks. Do you ever monitor the contents?"

Donnelly's eyes narrowed. "Short answer? No. But if you're looking to do a little illegal hauling, Ms. Meikle, you'd better go somewhere else for your truck. I don't have anything available right now."

It was clear the interview was over. In case there might be any lingering doubt about that, Donnelly got up and held the door open for me. I looked at the Rolex on his wrist. "That's a nice little car parked outside. Does it belong to you?" I got my foot out of the way half a second before Donnelly banged the door shut.

"Monday," I explained to his startled secretary. "It hits some people harder than others." She gave me a doubtful smile. Her switchboard had already lit up, indicating that Donnelly was on the line calling someone.

CHAPTER **TWENTY-TWO**

I decided I had nothing to lose by checking out the office of Mr. T. David Beare. Laura had already provided me with the address, the top floor of a two-story house. I found it in a section of the city heavily hit by renovators enamoured of sandblasting, bleached oak, and plant hangers. The results were not unattractive, but I doubted that the original working class owners would have recognized their erstwhile homes.

Beare Investments Ltd., or its decorator, favoured dark green paint, oak trim, and coordinating fabrics on chairs and windows. The halogen lighting was easy on the eyes. The room was very attractive and it showed not a whit of individual taste.

A discreet bell chimed as I went in. When no one answered it immediately, I took the opportunity to poke my nose into the two offices that opened off the reception area. Both were empty. One was apparently used as a conference room, the other, presumably, was the sanctum of T. David Beare himself. It didn't look as though he had been in to do any work recently.

A third door opened and I found myself face to face with the Dragon Lady I assumed had stonewalled Laura on the phone.

In looks she lived up to advance billing. She was rail thin, very tall, with a surprising mane of greying hair and penetrating eyes. She looked about as flexible as a piece of pressed steel. As she closed the door behind her, I caught a glimpse of an elegantly appointed bathroom. At least she's human, I thought, putting on an ingenuous smile.

Sighting me down her substantial nose, the Dragon Lady fired out the required, "May I help you?" Her tone suggested it was doubtful.

"I certainly hope so," I said, handing her my business card. "I'd like to see Mr. Beare." She took my card without touching my fingers, giving the impression of one who takes pains to avoid physical contact.

"You have no appointment." It was not a question.

"No, but . . ."

She was impervious. "Mr. Beare does not see anyone without an appointment."

"I see. Well, then, I'd like to make an appointment. How about this afternoon?"

"I'm afraid that would be quite impossible."

"Tomorrow?"

She shook her head.

"Suppose you tell me when Mr. Beare might be available."

"Mr. Beare is away at present. He is not expected back until the end of the month at least," she said with a certain amount of satisfaction.

"Does Mr. Beare have an assistant?"

"I am Mr. Beare's assistant," she replied, making no move to introduce herself further.

Momentarily defeated, I glanced around the office for inspiration. The main door was still ajar. A modest plaque on it bore the name "Beare Investments Limited" in fine gold letters.

"An uncle of mine died recently and left me quite a bit of money," I said, inventing a relative. "I need some advice on how to invest it."

The Dragon Lady's smile was frosty. "Mr. Beare does not handle individual accounts," she said. "He deals in corporate investments only." The pride in her voice was unmistakable, and so was the snub.

"Really?"

"Really."

"That's too bad. I've heard some good things about Mr. Beare. I was really hoping he could help me."

The assistant said nothing. What would Sam Spade or Philip Marlowe do now, I wondered. Something slick no doubt, something smooth that would gain them access to Beare's files and ultimately to Beare himself.

"Do you mind if I use your bathroom?"

The Dragon Lady was clearly taken aback, but even she could hardly refuse such a fundamental demand of nature. In the reception area, the bell chimed again. A pudgy young man entered, toting what looked like a large suitcase and wearing an ingratiating smile. He looked like a service rep of some kind. That should keep the Dragon Lady busy for a few minutes. I smiled winningly and entered door number three. The lock snicked behind me.

It wasn't a bathroom. It was a work of art: plush carpet, plush towels, plush bum wipe too. A body could sit comfortably enthroned in there for quite a while perusing the magazines so thoughtfully provided by the management. I wondered if the Dragon Lady was in charge of subscriptions. I doubted it. *Esquire* and *Cosmopolitan* hardly seemed in her line. She had the untouched look of an ice maiden. Fire may well have raged beneath the surface chill, but it would take a brave man to stir the coals.

I had hoped that the bathroom might have a connecting door to Beare's office and I wasn't disappointed. I opened it a crack and peered through. The main door to Beare's office stood ajar, but the Dragon Lady and the service rep were huddled together over the computer in the far corner and I managed to ease the main door fractionally more shut without attracting their attention.

Unfortunately, my unauthorized search of the premises ended almost as soon as it began. Everything was locked, desk, drawers, filing cabinets—even the tall, standing coat cupboard in the corner. Was this guy Beare paranoid or what? Did he think someone might want to steal his shoes? It's too bad none of the Ministry courses includes lock picking.

A big desk stood in front of the window. There was maybe an acre of workspace there, all of it empty, not so much as a paper clip littering its surface. I spared a thought for my own cluttered office. Beare's computer monitor angled across one corner of his desk, with a sliding shelf for the keyboard underneath. On the right was a disk storage box. Unfortunately, like everything else in the room, it was locked.

Grouped across the room from the desk were a couch, two chairs, and a bleached oak coffee table. Glossy newsletters were arranged on its glass top at precise right angles to the corners. I glanced over the titles, which were all the same. They were copies of the annual report for Beare Investments Ltd. Feeling slightly foolish, I picked one up and stuffed it under my sweater. There was no sense going away empty-handed, though I wasn't sure what good an annual report was going to do me, nor why I should feel it necessary to hide the thing. It was highly unlikely that "illegal dumping of toxic waste" would be listed on the statement of operations. Still, it helped me feel the part and so did remembering to flush the unused toilet on my way out of the washroom.

The Dragon Lady gave me a hard stare as I moved toward the door. I smiled and sent her a jaunty little wave, which she ignored. My card, emblazoned with the Ministry of Environment logo, still lay on her desk. I wondered if T. David Beare would ever see it. Given the overprotective attitude of his secretary, the odds were it would go out with the garbage at the end of the day.

CHAPTER **TWENTY-THREE**

I caught the first available flight back to Geddes Lake, putting in a quick call to Laura's office before I left. Tracy Semple told me she was still in court.

"She's got a client booked at four, Ms. Meikle, and she has a squash game at six. That's a long-standing date, she never misses it," Tracy warned, making it clear that I was not the exception to break the rule.

"That's okay, I'll call her again from home. Or she can call me."

There didn't seem to be much point in hanging around Toronto. I'd had enough of city life for a while and there was a pile of unfinished business on my office desk.

I arrived home to find the message light on my machine blinking. Neil Ewing had called, wanting to know if he could use my computer for a school project. "It'd be really cool to put some of those graphics you were showing me in. Some of the other kids are using computer stuff for theirs, the teacher says it's okay, so if it's okay with you, could I? I don't need it right away or anything, I have to do all the research part first, but maybe next week? Could you call me and let me know? Thanks, Charlie."

Smiling, I dialled the Ewings's number. Paul answered.

"Glad to hear you're back safe and sound," he said. "Did you find out anything useful?"

"Sort of, but not really."

"That sounds definite."

I explained the connection between Windrush, SOP, and Burden. "The linchpin seems to be this guy Beare, but I'm having a hell of a time locating him."

"It sounds like you stirred the pot pretty thoroughly. Maybe something will bubble over."

"Yeah," I said. "Maybe. It works that way in detective fiction anyway. Meanwhile, how's the clean up going?"

"About what you'd expect. A lot of political posturing, a lot of busy technicians. So far we've managed to keep it pretty quiet, but I don't know how long that's going to last. Walt Neely from the *Globe* was nosing around town yesterday trying to sniff out a story, so obviously the rumours have started to fly. There's certainly nothing else newsworthy around this place."

"No? What about the bear carcasses? Why doesn't someone enlighten Neely on that score? A nice centre-spread on profiting from poaching would look good in the Saturday edition."

Paul sounded tired. "Hell, nobody cares, Charlie, you know that. The only time people get up in arms over wildlife is when the Natural Resources guys have to organize a cull."

"The cute furry-burries helpless in the face of the big, bad 'govermint.'"

"Exactly. Some days I feel like I'm beating my head against a wall with this stuff."

"I know what you mean. You got anything on for tomorrow? How 'bout a beer at The Angler after work?"

"Sounds good."

"Great. Don't hang up. Is Neil around? He left a message on my machine."

I talked to Neil for a few minutes about his project. He figured he'd have all his research done by the following Sunday, so we made a date for that afternoon. I pencilled it in on my calendar, noting all the blank spaces between now and then. I knew the in-basket on my desk was full of ways to fill them. They could wait 'til tomorrow. I grabbed a bottle of wine from the fridge and invited myself for a visit with Irene Creighton.

She greeted me like an old friend. With relief, I noted that her shakiness had subsided and I guessed that the shock of Luther's death had passed, though clearly she still missed him. I asked if she planned to get another dog.

She shook her head. "Not just yet. But soon, I think. I'll be ready soon."

We raised our glasses to the picture of Luther now standing in pride of place on the mantle. I settled more comfortably in the chair, stretching my legs out to the fire. A half-finished crossword puzzle lay on the table beside me. I glanced at it idly. It was one of those cryptic puzzles where some of the answers are so obscure as to be practically meaningless. Mrs. Creighton didn't seem to be having any trouble with it.

"It must be one of those left brain, right brain things," I said. "I've never been able to get my head around them. Let's see. Ten down. 'He has a model attitude. Starts with a *p*.'" I sipped the wine while I thought about it. "Paragon? No, that can't be it. The answer's only got six letters."

"What about 'poseur'?" Mrs. Creighton suggested after a minute.

Dutifully I filled in the letters. "See what I mean? I only

thought of model as meaning perfect."

Mrs. Creighton smiled. "So many words have more than one meaning. It's what makes them interesting. Like people. Everyone has more than one side. That way they can fit into more than one context."

I threw another log on the fire, reminding myself to get busy pretty soon restocking my own woodpile. Mrs. Creighton wandered out to the kitchen, returning a few minutes later with a plate of crackers and some old cheddar cut in chunks. She put it down on a low table between us.

"I overheard some gossip the other day that you might find interesting, Charlie."

"Oh? What's that?" I asked, idly stretching out a hand to the plate of food.

"Larry Taylor has disappeared."

I stared. "Since when?"

"Last Thursday. Rumour has it Dorrie kicked him out of her house. There's no end to the speculation as to why."

I froze, cracker and cheese hovering mid-way between the plate and my mouth. There was little doubt in my mind as to why, or who Larry would hold responsible. Carefully, I put the cracker back down on the plate.

"Where did you hear this?" I asked.

"At the hairdresser."

I looked at her with some suspicion. The neatly plaited grey hair looked exactly the same as it had the last time I saw her. "The hairdresser?" I echoed. "You went to the hairdresser?"

"Actually, I treated myself to a spa day." She added

with some asperity, "You needn't look so surprised. After what happened to Luther, I was feeling kind of worked up, so I thought I'd give the mud wraps a try." Her lips twitched. "At my age, there aren't too many other options left for stress relief."

"Apart from brandy," I said.

"Which is certainly cheaper than the spa," she said.

"But apparently not as useful."

Irene Creighton giggled. And for a moment she was not a woman approaching eighty, but a girl of eighteen. "Just like in the movies," she said with some satisfaction. "You can learn an awful lot by spending an afternoon at the spa."

I wagged my finger at her. "You be careful. I'm not kidding, now. Getting anywhere near Larry Taylor is definitely not a good idea."

"Yes, well, he's gone now, monster truck and all. How long he'll stay away is another matter. I suppose it depends on how much Dorrie paid him to go."

"You think his mother gave him money to leave town?"

"I doubt," she said slowly, "that his mother is ready to abandon him completely. Whatever he may have done."

Flames danced lightly over the firewood; ash sifted down between the fingers of the grate.

"Did you know he hits her?"

"Yes."

"And she lets him."

"Yes."

"Why?"

Irene Creighton shrugged. "Because he's her son.

Because she loves him. Because she doesn't know how to make him other than what he is."

I shook my head in bewilderment. "Then why kick him out now?"

She gave me a level look. "Maybe someone else finally stood up to him and showed her it could be done."

"Is that what the gossips say?"

"Something like that."

I stared into the fire. For the past few days, I had succeeded in pushing the scene in Dorrie Taylor's kitchen to the back of my mind. Now it rushed to the forefront, swamping me with dread.

I could have stopped Larry Taylor that night without burning him. Had already done it, in fact. Then from God knows what abyss of the soul had come that driving need for revenge. I had wanted to hurt the son of a bitch, not just for Dorrie's sake, but for the sake of all the victims, animal and human, of abusers like Larry. What frightened me most was that in the moment when I could have stopped it, I had allowed the impulse to punish to override restraint. If Larry now held me accountable for his recent homelessness, I had only myself to blame.

As I headed home, I tried to convince myself the shiver up my spine was from the cold, not fear.

CHAPTER **TWENTY-FOUR**

Les Mills was waiting when I got out of my car. He hurled himself at me from the dark like an avenging fury, clawing at my face and shrieking obscenities as I fumbled with my keys.

It was midnight. I was bone weary and totally unprepared for his leap from nowhere. He got in a couple of good punches to my arm before I managed to push him off.

Since Les is a few inches shorter and maybe twenty pounds lighter than I am, holding him back was no major accomplishment. I gave him a little shake, and held him pinned to the wall, legs flailing, while he articulated his feelings.

"You dirty bitch!" he screamed. "Interferin' no good spy! Breakin' in to people's homes. Breakin' up their fam'lies. Who the hell gave you the right? Who the fuck do you think you are, eh? Govermint flunky! Goddamn govermint spy!"

I let him rant, waiting for his rage to wear itself out. My arm ached and I knew there would be bruises there tomorrow, where he'd landed his quick one-two. It's a good thing they always seem to go for the right arm. A trickle of blood on my cheek told me he'd connected there as well. Anger spurted. Hell and damnation, I thought, I have been here before and I am not going to take this shit from anyone ever again. I wanted to pound the bejesus out of the scrawny little runt in front of me. I took several deep breaths and gave him another little shake.

"Okay, Les, okay, you've had your say, and you've landed a couple of punches. Now how about calling it a night. I don't want to have to call the cops on you."

"That's right, call the cops, you gutless . . ."

"Dad!" Dorrie Taylor's voice cut sharply through the night.

Her father stopped in mid-epithet, mouth agape, eyes rounded in astonishment at his daughter's unexpected appearance on the scene. My expression was probably just as stunned, but I wasn't at all unhappy to see her. I let go of the father and gave the daughter a tired smile. She ignored me completely.

In a hard little voice she said, "I warned you, Dad. I told you to leave Ms. Meikle out of it. What happened with Larry is not her fault."

"Like hell it isn't!" Les insisted. "If this interferin' bitch hadn't a come pokin' her nose in where it didn't belong . . ."

"What, Dad?" Dorrie said acidly. "What would have happened? I'll tell you what. Larry would've beat on me some more and I would've ended up in the emergency again. Spinning another one about a fall down the stairs. And you, what would you have done, Dad? You would have made excuses for him."

The bitterness of her words made me wince. This was not a scene I wanted to witness, though for all the notice Dorrie and Les took of me, I might not have been there.

"Dorrie . . ." the old man whined, "you got to understand. The boy . . ."

Dorrie snapped, "He's not a boy, Dad. He's a man, full grown. He's got to learn to take a man's responsibility for what he does."

Les pleaded mutely, watery-eyed. Dorrie wavered for a moment, then her expression hardened again.

She enunciated her next words very clearly, giving each one equal weight. "He has no right. He has no right to hit me. No right to kill them bears so he can buy a truck. He is not above the law."

I looked at Les, sagging against the wall, refusing now to meet the eyes of the woman standing so straight before him in the moonlight. I watched the swagger desert him, the self-righteousness dissolve to reveal the pathetic old man beneath. I wished myself anywhere but there.

Dorrie, too, it seemed. She silently took her father's arm and with barely a glance at me, led him to her car. It was parked right behind mine in the drive, but the sound of her arrival had been drowned in her father's outburst. I watched her noiseless departure with a mixture of admiration and regret and silently wished her well.

The emotional scene had left me too keyed up for sleep. I wandered aimlessly around the house, restlessly thumbing through old magazines and zapping through a blur of TV trivia. I poured myself a generous hit of Scotch and unpacked my travelling bag by the simple expedient of throwing everything into the laundry bin. The annual report I had filched from Beare's office fluttered out and landed on the floor. I leafed through it from back to front, scanning the columns of figures without any real understanding of what I was looking at. Income seemed to have increased substantially over the past year, but the cash flow summary was gibberish to me, and I found no direct references to either SOP or Burden Transport, except a listing as related companies. The blurb at the front of the report was slightly more interesting, only because it was accompanied by a head and shoulders photo of the president and CEO , Mr. T. David Beare himself. At last, I had a face to connect with the name.

It wasn't a bad face as far as I could tell. Most of it was covered by a closely trimmed black beard, the full head of hair above styled to executive perfection. Though it's difficult to judge a man's expression when his mouth is obscured by facial hair, the roundness of Beare's cheeks suggested he was smiling. Since the photo was in black and white, I had no way of knowing what colour his eyes were, but from the lightness of his skin tone, I guessed at blue.

T. David Beare. According to the caption below the picture, the T. stood for Theodore. I laughed out loud. I bet the guy started going by his middle name around the age of six. His mother probably found the name Teddy Beare incredibly cute, but it's the kind of thing that's tough to defend on the playground.

In his photo the president of Beare Investments Ltd. was soberly attired in business drab, a self-important tie held in place by an oblong stickpin whose design seemed out of keeping with the rest of his feet-on-the-ground image. I wouldn't have thought a man choosing that tie would elect to adorn it with a bird in flight. It was imagery more suited to a free spirit type like Frank Dennison. In fact, he had been wearing something very similar on his leather vest.

I grabbed a magnifying glass and turned on another lamp. There was no question about it. The same long-legged bird that had been taking flight on Dennison's jacket was soaring over the stripes of David Beare's tie.

I thought of my friend, Jan Somers, who was responsible for all the actors's make-up and hairstyles at the Geddes Lake Little Theatre. While I helped build sets, she designed faces, and one afternoon she'd plunked me down in a chair for a demonstration of her wizardry.

"It doesn't take as much as you'd think," she'd said, "to alter someone's appearance. Now just hold still for a minute."

She had been armed with a curling iron and I'd watched her approach with a certain amount of anxiety, but it had been an instructive quarter hour. The fuzzy head and newly bespectacled face that eventually stared back at me from the mirror bore little resemblance to the one I was used to seeing. Jan had used no make-up, no false teeth or hair, but the result was startling. Instant anonymity.

I squinted at the photo in front of me, mentally comparing the face of David Beare with what I remembered of Frank Dennison. The beard would hide the acne scars of course, but beyond that the shape of the face was the same and the skin tone looked right. I had no doubt at all about the eye colour.

Jan had told me that simple changes are usually the most effective. She'd been right. In this case, shave the beard, let the hair grow out a little, vary the wardrobe, and there you were. No wonder David Beare was so hard to find. He'd become Frank Dennison.

CHAPTER **TWENTY-FIVE**

The question of what to do next nagged like an incipient toothache. I doodled on a scratchpad while I thought about it.

To my mind, there was plenty of evidence linking David Beare, aka Frank Dennison, to the Windrush Mine and it was clear now why "Dennison" had never confronted Beare with the problems there—what would he have told himself? I knew what would happen if I passed the information on to the authorities now. Once the press got wind of it, the story would embarrass Save Our Planet and maybe even cause it to fold completely. Without their trusted leader, I didn't think the SOP groupies could survive. With a push in the right direction, any enterprising journalist could expose Teddy Beare as chief crook and garbage dumper. But as a murderer?

Idly, I tapped my pencil against the side of the desk while I studied the face in the photograph again. It looked soft rather than decisive. No doubt my imagination was coloured by long exposure to Hollywood cliché, but it was not the face of a man I could envision killing anyone. Covert dumping was one thing; murder was something else. He might have hired someone for the job but I didn't really think so. He hadn't impressed me as that much of a risk taker. Teddy Beare was no Don Corleone.

Suddenly tired of the staccato rhythm of the pencil, I tossed the pencil aside and got up to put on a CD. I was just popping one out of its case when it occurred to me that there were a couple of other possibles worth examining for the role of murderer: Matt Donnelly and the Dragon Lady. Donnelly had struck me as the type who would go far to protect a Porsche lifestyle. The Dragon Lady I was less sure about, though my own recent brush with the darker motivations of the soul made me unwilling to dismiss her out of hand. Both were close to Beare. Had one of them gone to Jim's cabin, perhaps at Beare's request, to find out what the old man knew, and maybe buy him off? I could imagine how that would have gone over with Jim. I could see an argument developing down by the lake. And then what? An impatient shove? A push to get the point across? Jim might have slipped and fallen, but someone had deliberately let him drown and had then staged an accident scene. I wondered if the same person had later staged one for me.

For the next few days I chased the possibilities like a hamster on a wheel, creating a flurry of mental activity but making no forward progress.

Office hours were filled with endless paperwork and phone calls. Lacking any fresh evidence, the poaching investigation had virtually ground to a halt. The fact that not a single dead bear had been found since Larry Taylor had left town led to some fairly obvious conclusions, though it would have been nice to nail the sucker firmly to the wall. Curly and Moe steadfastly denied any knowledge of their buddy's whereabouts. Not knowing where Les Mills's boy was made me very nervous indeed. I stumbled through a good part of the day with one eye over my shoulder, wary of attack from Larry or his grandfather.

Joan reminded me we were expecting visitors from Dorset. Ministry courses in everything from law enforcement to wilderness survival are taught at the Outdoor Ed Centre there and we had all attended them, but it was unusual that one of their number should journey up to Geddes Lake. I had visions of some hotshot investigator dragging us out for yet another search of the ground we had combed so fruitlessly for the past month.

Nonetheless, I took the time to rebraid my hair and straighten my clothes, enjoying the subtle transformation of self that grooming allows. I don't wear much makeup, but a little mascara and blush work wonders on my self-esteem. I hate facing the world with all my blemishes exposed.

On my way to the conference room, I stopped to reload the coffee maker and was startled to find a dog guarding the entrance to the little kitchen. He was lying in that posture dogs adopt when they are relaxed, but alert. His tongue looked very pink against the glossy black coat, and his sides heaved gently with the measured rhythm of his panting. He didn't stir at my approach, but he watched me intently, the grin widening on his big Lab face as I stooped to stroke the downy spot between his ears. His tail thumped twice gently and he rolled slightly to expose his belly.

A male voice said, "Don't let that cream puff fool you. Any minute now he'll jump up and attack."

"He certainly looks vicious." I bestowed a final pat before looking up. "How do you ever hold him back?"

"Special training. Good boy, Logan."

Despite his banter, there was nothing soft about the

man who stood beside me, fishing in his pocket for a bone-shaped crunchie. He was dressed in jeans and a sweater, and although his head was bare, he looked as though a hat would suit him, not a baseball cap, but a broad-brimmed slouch, like cowboys wear. He had an untidy thatch of thick dark hair, an outdoor tan, and blue eyes that met mine in frank appraisal.

He held out his hand. "Kevin Shakespeare. Pleased to meet you."

"Hi, Kevin. Charlotte Meikle," I said. "Charlie."

He smiled and dropped my hand. "Thank you."

"What for? Telling you my nickname?"

"That too, but actually, I meant for not making a crack about the bard. You'd be surprised how many people can't resist."

"Well, it's not as if you'd named your dog Hamlet . . ."

At that point, Jeff, Bob, and our area supervisor, Grant Lubitsch, crowded up, fussing over the dog and making introductions. Smirking, Jeff said, "Pleased to meet you, William." Kevin Shakespeare looked resigned and I laughed out loud.

When the coffee was ready, everyone grabbed a mug and headed down the hall. Logan padded after us to resume his guard post outside the door. Our conference room had originally been furnished with a plain deal table and chairs, but Joan had objected to its functional sterility and had spent a couple of Saturdays transforming it into a comfortable meeting place. A stunning array of wildlife posters brightened the walls, and cushions in a pattern of forest green and yellow now padded the chairs, making it possible to sit for longer than ten minutes without fidgeting. The focal point of the room was the table, where Joan's artistry showed to its best advantage. She had contrived a fantastic underwater scene of glowing cutthroat and rainbow trout, bright pumpkinseeds, and spawning red salmon, their colours vibrant against a dark blue background. Once it was finished, the mural had been laminated to protect the paintwork, and it now provided a unique, durable, and very attractive workspace.

Grant explained why Kevin Shakespeare and Logan were there.

"He can find a lost hat, a knife, concealed fish, deer meat—anything that might have been stashed, hidden, or thrown away. When it comes to following a scent, he's unbeatable," Grant said. "Or so I understand."

"You make him sound like a cross between Rin Tin Tin and Lassie," said Jeff. "He doesn't look that impressive to me."

We all looked at the dog. Logan yawned and settled himself more comfortably, head between his paws.

Kevin was unperturbed. "I've had this fellow for two years," he said. "I take him everywhere with me. I use him a lot for PR in schools—the kids love him. He looks harmless, I know, but he's pulled my ass out of the fire more than once and he can follow the trail of anything you want, from a man to a moose. Grant thought he might be useful in running your bear poacher to ground."

We agreed it couldn't hurt to try. If Logan was as clever as Kevin said, he just might nose out something our lesser human senses had missed. Jeff and Bob were knocking off early. They had poacher duty again tonight, so it fell to me to show Kevin and Logan the bear sites.

The dog proved his worth at the second one. He sniffed around the carcass, already picked nearly clean by scavengers, moving away from it in slowly widening circles, his nose never far off the ground. About ten feet away he paused, then poked his head into a pile of leaves, shuffling them up with his nose. Logan inched further in under some prickly gorse until only his hindquarters were visible and I saw his tail start to wag more energetically as he scrabbled excitedly in the underbrush. He emerged triumphant a minute later, with a hunk of brown leather clutched gently in his teeth. I'd always heard that retrievers had soft mouths, but I was unprepared for the feather light brush of his muzzle against my hand as he dropped his prize into it. It was the sheath from a hunting knife.

"Good boy, good dog!"

Logan politely accepted a handful of biscuits as his due.

The dark brown leather was still stiff with newness. The blade that had fitted it was broad and relatively short and would have been useful in gutting a carcass. Still holding it flat, I turned the sheath over in my hand. It was an unremarkable piece, of a kind sold by the thousands in outdoor stores across the country. There were no initials or identifying marks carved into it, which was a pity, but there might still be a chance for fingerprints, so I dropped it carefully into the polythene bag Kevin was holding out to me and zipped it shut.

"Our first solid clue," I said. "I hope it does us some good."

"D'you have any suspects?"

I told him about Larry and the stooges.

"The circumstantial evidence certainly points their way," he agreed. "Maybe the sheath will help tie it up for you."

It was six when we got back to town, and I suggested a beer at The Angler. To my surprise, the parking lot was nearly full, and from the sound of things, a party was in progress inside. Leaving the dog in Kevin's Outback, we elbowed our way through a carnival crowd toward a table on the far side of the room, tucked in behind the door to the kitchen. As we sat down, a loud chorus of "We are the champions" echoed around the room.

"What's going on?" I yelled to a passing waitress.

"Somebody bought the Limberlost," she shouted back. "Word just came down."

"American?"

"No!" she screamed. "Canadian. Some big time investor from Toronto. He's going to put in some new management, but all these guys," she gestured at the revellers, "get to keep their jobs."

She plunked down a couple of draft. "On the house. I need to get me some ear protectors."

"We are the champions?" said Kevin. "I don't get it. Why not 'he's a jolly good fellow'?"

I shrugged. "Most of the guys here play in the softball league. It's the only song they all know."

We watched the waitress thread her way back toward the bar, dispensing free draft as she went.

"The owner here is very generous," said Kevin.

"He knows who his customers are. As long as the Limberlost stays in business, so will The Angler."

The draft was warm. Given the number of celebrants in the room, the bartender had probably run out of cold beer some time ago.

"Are you staying at Grant's?" I asked.

Kevin nodded. "He and I go way back. This'll be a nice chance to catch up. His kids are dying to see the dog, but I understand the oldest girl has allergies, so Logan will have to rough it on the porch for one night. I expect the cold shoulder all day tomorrow as payback."

"He's a lovely animal. Was he hard to train?"

"No. I taught him basic obedience myself and then I took him to the OPP canine unit in Brampton. Labs are right up there on the doggy intelligence scale and since he's a retriever, tracking came pretty easily to him."

"He sure did a great job today. Thanks a lot."

"Glad to be of service."

We sipped our warm beer. Kevin palmed a handful of peanuts.

"Are you driving back tomorrow?"

"There's someone I want to look up first, a guy I met a few years ago who helped us put together a program in forensic accounting. I understand he's retired up here now and I'd like to stop in and say hello while I'm here. His name's Jim Griffith. Have you ever heard of him?"

Something of the shock I felt must have shown in my face.

"What's the matter?"

"Jim's dead."

"Really? I'm sorry to hear that. He was a great guy. What was it, a heart attack?"

"No. He drowned."

Kevin was startled. "Drowned? How did that happen?"

I outlined the circumstances that had led to the coroner's ruling of accidental death.

"Hmm. Jim must have aged a lot since I knew him. He was always so organized, it's hard to imagine someone that competent being so careless."

"I thought so, too."

Kevin raised his eyebrows in a gesture that invited me to continue. I studied him briefly. A trained investigator, he would be an ideal sounding board. He listened attentively while I sketched the events of the past few weeks for him, omitting the personal and presenting, as clearly as I understood them, the facts of what I called the toxic dumping case.

"How far have they gotten with the clean up?"

I shrugged. "They've done a lot of testing to see how far the contamination extends. And of course they've resealed the drums and removed them. Paul says they're thinking of digging a trench, you know, to interrupt the flow into the lake. Whether they'll go as far as to layer the lake itself with silt, I don't know. It's an expensive undertaking and Finger Lake is just not that important in any economic or even recreational sense. They're more likely to just close it off."

Kevin sighed. "What a waste."

The waitress cruised past our table, offering more draft. We declined. A new wave of celebrants had just come in and the volume was rising to intolerable. Kevin looked at his watch.

"I have to mosey," he said. "Grant's expecting me for dinner at seven."

"Is it that late already?" I pushed back my chair. "I have to get going too."

We negotiated a more or less straight path to the door and the quiet outside.

"My eardrums thank you," I said. "And I thank you too, for listening."

"I wish there was some way I could help," Kevin said. "If Jim's death wasn't an accident, I'd like to help you prove it. Do you have some time tomorrow? I wouldn't mind going out to his place to look around a little. Maybe Logan can find us another clue."

CHAPTER **TWENTY-SIX**

Naturally, the hardware store was closed. The number of empty parking stalls out front should have clued me, but I got all the way to the front door before I noticed the sign, "Gone Hunting, Back Monday." Other stores undoubtedly sell tap washers, but I was so used to buying everything at Young's that I didn't even bother to look. I merely resigned myself to another night with the washcloth.

I had just enough time to eat a quick sandwich and read over my mail before I was due for rehearsal at the theatre. Apart from a phone bill and the National Geographic, there was a letter from my mother, full of aimless chatter about the everyday doings of my sister's family. She had enclosed a couple of snapshots taken at Emily's seventh birthday party. I had sent a balloon-o-gram. Half way through the party, a clown had arrived at the front door bearing a huge bouquet of helium balloons. Emily had accepted them with squeals of delight and the little girls had spent the afternoon batting them around the house like volleyballs, while the clown twisted long, skinny ones into a kaleidoscope of animal shapes. Emily herself had scratched me a thank you at the bottom of the page. She had tried to save me a piece of cake, she said, but Buster had eaten it. I laughed. Buster was her stuffed bear.

Rehearsal was at seven-thirty. No one was ever late; Geddes Lake Little Theatre productions had a reputation for near-professional quality, a reflection of the attitude of the cast. Tonight we were working on the scene where Eliza Doolittle has just mastered her vowels. As housekeeper, it was my job to persuade her to bed when she could have danced all night, which made a nice change from bar fights and bear carcasses.

Afterward, Jan showed me the wig she wanted me to wear, a sensible looking arrangement of grey hair neatly done up in a bun, without a vestige of style.

"I can't wear this," I said.

"Why not? It's perfect. It'll make you look at least sixty, and with the glasses," she unfolded a pair of wire rims, "you'll be just right."

"But how am I going to get all this hair up under a wig?"

She eyed my thick braid. "We'll find a way." She laid the trappings of my character back in a box labelled with my name. "Do you have time for a cup of tea?"

Tea with Jan had become part of the routine of rehearsal. She lived in one side of a duplex, a couple of blocks from the auditorium and within walking distance of her office. Her own face and hair reflected none of the cosmetic artistry she so cleverly applied to others. She always seemed rather prim and dry, her scent a bit musty, like herbs that have been kept too long. Though only in her early fifties, Jan was already talking eagerly of her plans for retirement, as though she would, on the appointed day, suddenly break out like a butterfly from its cocoon. By profession, she was a software analyst, an occupation that made her sideline seem almost medieval by contrast. Jan was an herbalist. In an earlier era, she would have been burned at the stake as a witch, but now she enjoyed a modest reputation as an amateur naturopath. Her plant experiments had transformed the sunroom into a chimerical greenhouse that made me think of hobbits and Middle Earth.

"I've come up with a new one," Jan said, as she laid out teacups and spoons. "It has a chamomile base, but I've added a touch of something else. See what you think of it."

I dipped a slice of lemon in my cup, a habit Jan had tried to break, saying I spoiled the drink before even tasting it, but I found a hint of lemon always improved the flavour of Jan's original teas, and this blend was no different.

I said, "You know, if you wanted to create something really useful, you'd develop an herb that could prove whether someone is guilty of a crime. It would save investigators a lot of hassle running around looking for evidence. If you suspected someone, all you'd have to do is wave the herb in front of their nose or something and they'd confess. Or maybe the herb could just change colour if they were guilty, or burst into flower if they were not."

"Apparently there already is such a thing."

"You mean the truth serum they use in spy stories?"

"No, no, an actual plant, called the Calabar bean. It comes from West Africa. They use the alkaloid to produce physostigmine."

"Eye drops?" I said.

Jan nodded. "According to superstition, the Calabar bean, or the 'ordeal bean' as it's called, is supposed to be able to prove innocence or guilt. The accused party simply chews one up and swallows. If he's innocent, nothing happens."

"What happens if he's guilty?"

"He dies."

"That's convenient. We could do away with the whole penal system." I bit into an oatmeal cookie with a satisfying crunch and nodded enthusiastic approval. Jan hadn't added any strange flora to this recipe.

She smiled. "That would certainly help reduce the deficit, but you'd still be left with the moral problem. After all, what is guilt or innocence?"

"I don't think there's any doubt about that," I said. "It's a question of right and wrong, good versus evil."

"Yes, but that's my point. Definitions of good and evil vary from one century to the next." She indicated her herbarium. "This is a case in point. No, what your ordeal bean would probably be testing is a only a sense of guilt or innocence, so it would have no value as a test at all."

"I don't see why not."

"Look at it this way. Someone thinks he has a divine calling to murder whores, or pimps . . ."

"Or poachers . . ."

"Whatever rouses his moral indignation. He commits what you consider a guilty act, but what he considers an innocent one. How would the ordeal bean react?"

I said, "Surely anyone who murders someone or rapes them, or hurts them in any way, must have some feelings of guilt."

"I don't think so. I think there are plenty of people with no conscience whatsoever."

On Wednesday morning, Laura called.

"How was the squash game?" I asked.

"Huh. I got my ass kicked. Patty's a really great player and I just wasn't on."

Laura made that little throat clearing sound people make when they're slightly embarrassed.

"Mark called me Sunday night."

"Don't tell me."

"He wanted to get together and renew old acquaintance."

"Mm. And you said?"

"Three guesses. The funny thing is, I thought I'd be ecstatic if he ever called me again, and when he finally did, I didn't feel anything. Not happy, not sad, not flattered, not angry, nothing. The big zero. I told him I wasn't interested."

"Did he accept that?"

"Are you kidding? Guys like Mark Dyment never accept rejection. Their egos won't allow for it. He told me and I quote, I was the 'most fucked up broad he'd ever known.' He said I should get some counselling to help liberate the inner me."

I laughed. "What did you say?"

"I told him I already spent twelve hours a day in counselling and didn't think I could cope with more liberation than that."

"Did he get the joke?"

"No, I think his sense of humour is in a permanent state of collapse."

I laughed again.

"Anyway," Laura said, "on to things that really matter. What's happening at your end?"

"I paid a visit to the Burden Transport people on Monday morning."

"Really? How did you make out? Did you find any

obvious links to the elusive David Beare?"

"How likely," I asked her, "do you think it is that the manager—not the owner, mind you, just the manager—of a small to middling trucking company should be driving a brand new Porsche and wearing a gold Rolex?"

"You're not serious."

"Yes I am."

She was silent for a moment. "Does the rest of him match the toys?"

I shook my head, forgetting for the moment that she couldn't see me. "No, it seems to be surface flash only. He has a cheap haircut, no manicure."

"Now there's a telling indictment," Laura said dryly. "So you figure the flash is newly acquired?"

"Yeah, I do. Donnelly hasn't gotten over the urge to show off yet," I said.

"So," Laura said thoughtfully, "I'd say he's getting money, and lots of it, from a source unrelated to the day-to-day operations of the trucking company. With the ties Burden has to Beare, and Beare's links to Save Our Planet and the Windrush, it's a pretty safe bet Donnelly's either doing the hauling himself, or at the very least, turning a blind eye to the use of his trucks."

"The links are tighter than you think." I told her about the photograph in the annual report I had pilfered from Beare's office and my certainty that Beare and Donnelly were the same man.

There was a shocked exclamation at the other end of the line. "But why would he do that?"

I had spent a lot of time mulling that one over during the past couple of days.

"Suppose," I said, "that you inherit a very successful business empire from your father. Dad was a stand-up guy, a real go-getter and you take over feeling pretty smug about the good life you can lead and all the power you can wield."

"I'm in hog heaven."

"Exactly. You are enjoying life. And maybe you're having such a good time, that you get a little lazy and business starts to slide, or maybe you just haven't got what it takes the way your father did. Whatever the reason, things start going downhill in a big way and the money is no longer rolling in. What do you do?"

I could visualize Laura, sitting at her desk, phone tucked into her shoulder, bottom lip caught between her teeth in concentration.

"I look for an infusion of capital," she said.

"From?"

I heard the shrug. "From a bank, I guess."

"And if the banks turn you down, as well they might, given your track record over the past few years?"

"Declare bankruptcy?"

"And admit defeat? Acknowledge that you're not the next Donald Trump, but, in fact, a failure?"

"Mm. I guess not. My ego must be pretty badly damaged though. So what do I do?"

"Cheat."

"Of course. Why didn't I think of that?"

"You have to have the bent for it," I said kindly.

"Bent is right. Are you planning to explain any of this to me?"

"Yes. If I am Teddy Beare . . ."

"Who?"

"Teddy Beare. Theodore Beare."

I heard her snort.

"That's actually the name he was born with," I said.

"No wonder he has an ego problem."

"Yes, well, as I was saying, if I am Teddy Beare, and I own an investment company which handles only my own failing investments, I might look to my other assets, namely a mine and a trucking company."

"But both of those assets have become liabilities," Laura objected.

"That's right, they have. But, I'm not totally devoid of imagination. I don't have to be hit over the head with a hammer to spot a trend. And when I look around my neighbourhood, what trends do I see? I see blue boxes and recycling depots and Save the Whales posters. I see T-shirts and buttons and magazines and people donating large sums of money to save the rainforest. On the other side of the street, I see businesses with a dwindling bottom line paying through the nose to dispose of their toxic wastes at approved dumpsites. And here I am with trucks to move stuff and an abandoned mine to store it in."

"But why all the Beare/Dennison role playing? Where does SOP fit in?"

"I think that was probably intended only as a stop-gap measure. Using old mine sites as storage facilities is under serious consideration by the powers that be. It's no accident that it's also a pet project of our favourite environmental group. If mine site storage is legalized, Beare can laugh all the way to the bank. But until it's legalized, he has to have somewhere to put all the money he's being paid to get rid of other people's garbage. Beare's existing companies had been failing for years; it would be hard to cover for a sudden jump in their income. He wouldn't want to draw any attention to himself, so he became Frank Dennison. What better depository could he have than a nice, tax-deductible donation to Save Our Planet? I bet the financial statements for SOP make for pretty interesting reading."

Laura said bitterly, "Jim must have figured it out, too. He knew who owned the Windrush; he would have tried to reach Beare. He must have talked to someone, somewhere, who decided to shut him up."

CHAPTER **TWENTY-SEVEN**

Kevin picked me up at one. Logan sat in the back seat, his front paws resting on top of the driver's seat, his head on Kevin's shoulder. I gave directions to Jim's cabin and we travelled the twenty miles to Finger Lake trading shop talk.

There had been frost on the scarlet leaves outside my window when I woke up that morning, but the sun had warmed the day, and though it was definitely sweater weather, it was too early to dig out my parka. Indian summer is always an unexpected treat, like finding another chocolate in the box when you thought it was empty.

The air was still and Finger Lake lay tranquil, showing no sign of the contamination infecting it. We went straight to the waterfront where Logan sniffed dutifully among the rocks and along the dock, but found nothing of particular interest. Then we headed back up to the cabin.

The outer door had been pulled half off its hinges, shredded screen hanging limply over its wooden frame. Intruders had smashed the lock on the main door by the simple expedient of shooting it out. Inside, the desecration was complete. Splintered furniture and slashed upholstery lay in scattered heaps around the room. Every piece of kitchen crockery had been hauled from the cupboards and smashed up against the fireplace. Jim had had no curtains, the isolation of the cabin being proof enough against prying eyes. I was surprised that the vandals had left the picture window intact, but Kevin pointed out broken glass would have been too noticeable. As it was, the window provided the perfect cover; from the lake all anyone would see was the reflection of the trees.

Logan nosed around the wreckage but I didn't expect him to come up with any clues. It was one thing to find a knife sheath in the underbrush, the smell of leather would attract a dog. But how could he possibly spot something that didn't belong here? The cabin was a total shambles. I was glad Jim wasn't there to see it.

My eye went to the space over the fireplace. Empty. Even the mounting hooks had been ruthlessly torn from the wall. I made a slow visual tour of the room, but nowhere could I see my old friend's treasured rainbow trout.

I remembered how meticulously Jim had prepared his prize, the painstaking removal of head and skin, the careful carving of the Styrofoam body form and moulding of the plaster cast around it. Once the cured skin had been fitted back over its form, I had watched him reinforce a torn fin web with tissue paper, using an artist's brush and oil paints to match the rainbow's original colours and a thin coat of varnish to protect them.

I heard a sound that was almost a sigh, an exhalation of breath on a dying fall. Kevin was standing at the doorway to Jim's bedroom and, as I moved toward him, he put out his arm and drew me aside as if to shield me from the sight.

Jim's rainbow trout lay shattered on the bed, the hammer used for its destruction tossed into a corner. Dozens of the flies Jim had laboured over had been jabbed into the fish's eye sockets, mouth, and gills, until it looked like some rotting thing, covered in maggots. Propped haphazardly around it were the PoachWatch posters. Large x's had been stencilled across them in feces, and beside them was a dried patch of what smelled like urine. Logan whined.

Anger twisted my gut and I began to shake. Very gently, Kevin turned me to face him and, wrapping both arms tightly around me, rocked me slowly back and forth until the shakes gave way to calm. After a minute or two, I was able to survey the room again.

"At least there's DNA evidence," I said.

"Plenty of fingerprints, too, I'd think. We'd better have the OPP take a look."

I nodded. I wasn't a crime scene investigator and neither was Kevin. Once the police had searched the cabin and collected their evidence, I'd hire someone in town to clean up the mess, someone to whom it would just be a job. I couldn't face it.

On the ride back to town Logan regarded me warily from the back seat. I sat sideways, facing Kevin, and my voice was overloud in the confines of the car. The dog's ears flattened.

"Larry Taylor might as well have left a calling card," I ranted. "Or signed his name in his own shit."

"You're sure it was him?" Kevin's tone was deliberately mild and, from the corner of my eye, I saw Logan relax fractionally in response to it. Taking a deep breath, I brought my voice down an octave.

"Nobody else would be stupid enough to leave all that evidence behind."

"Vandals?" Kevin suggested.

I shook my head. "They're pretty rare around here. We get the usual graffiti, broken glass and now and then somebody with a grievance will key someone else's car or lop the tops off their prize roses, but wrecking things just for the hell of it? We don't see much of that. Besides," I went on, "Larry had a motive. He hated the whole idea of PoachWatch. He saw it as an infringement of his right to hunt and kill whatever he wanted, whenever he wanted. Poor Jim. And that beautiful, beautiful fish." The end of my nose started to tingle, a sure sign I was about to cry. I pinched it hard, blinking back tears. "God, I hope Larry Taylor rots in hell."

My friendship with Jim had been common knowledge, and even if it weren't, my job was. Jim's cabin was in my territory; I would be keeping an eye on it as a matter of course. Larry knew I'd be the first one to see his handi-work. I had no doubt he had trashed the place to spite me. I shivered, remembering his promise to kill me. Naively, I had dismissed his threat as bluster and him as a drunken bully. I had even accosted him in his mother's kitchen. Now I wondered if he'd been to Finger Lake before, to try to persuade Jim—or intimidate him—into abandoning PoachWatch. Jim would have refused. Had Larry hit him and left him to drown? My stomach churned. I had a vivid memory of the look on Larry's face as he cradled the fingers I'd burned, and I hoped the OPP would find him fast.

Kevin and I filed statements at the police station. I was beginning to feel at home there, helping myself quite naturally to a disposable cup and some coffee. Paul and

I had recently spent the better part of an afternoon in this office, notifying the authorities of the illegal dumping at the Windrush Mine and establishing a liaison with the Ministry to effect the cleanup. Now I thought Constable Bourque might be interested in my theories on locating the mine's owner, who also happened to be the activist leader of an environmental group. There was scepticism in the officer's face as he took down what I had to say about Beare/Dennison, obvious disapproval in his pursed lips as he recorded the details of my visits to SOP and the Burden Transport offices. He was too professional to actually roll his eyes when I described the incident of the dog at the Windrush Mine, but disbelief hung heavy in the air, indicating that in this regard the elaborately staged scenario there had been successful. The part he did take seriously was less dependent on my word than on the well-documented and fingerprinted life history of Larry Taylor. Given the abundance of evidence at the cabin, it should be easy to tie that crime to Larry. I left the station with the reassurance that the police would be on the lookout for him. They extended only half-hearted thanks for my theory regarding the whereabouts of T. David Beare.

Somewhere between the raised eyebrows and pursed lips I made a decision not to mention any theories about Jim's death. If Constable Bourque wanted to treat me like a fool over Dennison and the toxic dump, so be it. That was a professional issue. Jim Griffith was a personal one.

Kevin and I went back to the office, where we explained all over again what had happened. Grant was tight-lipped, eyeing me with concern.

"I think maybe you should take a few days off, Charlie. This has been rough on you."

Uninvited, Kevin followed me home.

"Can I buy you some dinner?" he asked.

I hesitated.

"That's okay," he said. "Some other time."

"It's not that . . . it's just . . . I really don't feel like going out. D'you want to eat here?"

Logan pushed his way in first. Kevin muttered something about the damn dog forgetting all the manners he had worked so hard to instil, but the big Lab ignored him, nosing happily around the main floor before flopping down with a contented sigh by the window overlooking the woods.

Kevin made himself at home, too, opening a bottle of wine while I ransacked the kitchen for edibles.

"I wish I could stick around for a few days, Charlie, and lend you some moral support, but I'm in the middle of a contract right now. I only stopped at Geddes Lake as a favour to Grant. The thing I'm working on will take about a week—I could stop again on the way back. If you don't mind."

"It'd be nice to think we'll have all the answers by then."

I scrambled eggs into lopsided omelettes. Kevin went out to the car for a bowl of dog chow that Logan munched in the kitchen while Kevin and I took our plates into the living room. We ate sitting on low chairs by the fire. To my surprise, it felt homey and comfortable. My defensive radar had been set pretty high after Nicholas and I didn't often entertain men in my home. The wine might have made a difference.

Kevin talked a little about himself and more about his sons, Gregory and Alex, who lived with him most of the time, going to their mother in Vancouver for holidays and school breaks.

"Nicole and I met at university and we got married before we graduated. She was beautiful, and so much fun I wouldn't listen to my father when he told me I was marrying her with my eyes instead of my head. As it turned out, she wasn't the least bit interested in hearth and home. She didn't even really want the boys. So now she's out in Vancouver trying to become an actress."

There was no bitterness in his voice, no regret in his face. I had the impression that, when the break came, he had welcomed it as much as she. Having come out of the marriage with the boys, he considered himself the winner.

At eight-thirty, Neil Ewing knocked on the door.

"What are you doing out wandering around at this hour?" I demanded.

"Dad's waiting for me in the car," Neil said. "Hey, are you okay? Your face looks kind of funny."

"I'm fine," I said, casting a quick glance in the hall mirror. Maybe I was a little flushed. Blame it on the second bottle of wine.

Neil said, "I just wanted to pick up that book you said I could borrow. I need it for school tomorrow."

I'd promised to lend him a photographic essay of the Grand Canyon, which took no time at all to locate on the shelf, but instead of waiting by the door, Neil had followed me into the living room. He assessed Kevin

Shakespeare with frank curiosity. Kevin gravely offered his hand. Logan sniffed with polite interest, picking up the scent of Daisy and Donald.

"Nice dog," Neil said. "Is he smart?"

"He has his moments," Kevin said.

"I have dogs," Neil said.

"What kind?" Kevin said.

"They're goldens," Neil said.

"Family dogs," Kevin said.

I stifled a laugh. They seemed prepared to spend the rest of the evening discussing canines in two word sentences. Luckily, as Neil opened his mouth to respond, Paul tooted the horn to remind him that this was meant to be a flying visit only.

The evening dwindled with the fire. By ten, my head was getting too heavy for my neck and Kevin rose to leave. Logan had been snoring by the window, but as soon as Kevin moved, he came instantly awake. He made a beeline for the kitchen coming back a moment later with his empty food bowl in his mouth.

I laughed. "He's done this before."

At the door, I sleepily patted the dog and shook hands with Kevin. "Thanks again for the help."

"My pleasure. See you soon." He bent forward suddenly, kissed me lightly on the cheek, and was gone.

CHAPTER **TWENTY-EIGHT**

I decided not to take Grant up on his offer of time off. Feeling edgy and anxious over the events of the past week, I felt safer within the confines of familiar office routines.

Jeff had left a memo on my desk with "Do you believe this?" penned across it. I picked it up.

Near the mouth of the Posquatch River there was an old railroad bridge that had been built when Harry Geddes established his Golden Mile. The cement base of the bridge had created an insurmountable barrier for the migrating rainbow trout in the river. During their arduous swim upstream, the fish managed to overcome some very shallow water and a sharp climb over a cluster of rocks, but by the time they got to the dam, they didn't have the energy to fling themselves over it. Instinct told them that a mile upstream of the bridge, richly gravelled spawning beds awaited, and they milled around in the deep pool at the base of the dam, gathering their strength for the leap. A few made it, but most didn't.

The deep pool became a favourite hangout for poachers. They came out after dark, like ghouls, with their flashlights and their dip nets and their spears, to haul the fish from the water, sometimes with the eggs streaming out of them. The Rod and Gun Club tried to help out by scooping the spawning fish from the pool in nets and lugging them up past the dam. A couple of the members tried to build their own fish ladder, but it was too narrow and too steep for success. Most of the rainbows couldn't find it, and those that did couldn't get more than half way up. The Ministry of Natural Resources had finally stepped in and, after years of patient negotiation with the railroad, created a two level terrace beside the bridge. The memo in front of me advised that the railroad was now shutting down the bridge. We could just as easily have poked a hole in the bottom and let the fish swim under the damn thing.

Grant was busy soliciting support for the idea of our office acquiring a dog like Logan. Everyone agreed that having an animal like him around would be useful, not only as an aid to investigation, but as a deterrent in a threatening situation. Confrontations with lawbreakers always held the potential for violence, which was why we conducted our poacher patrols in pairs. In the wake of Logan's successful visit Grant had done a little creative bookkeeping and decided the office could afford to hire a four-legged deputy. The only drawback seemed to be the question of who would be responsible for the dog. Grant was out because of his daughter's allergies. Bob declined on the basis of the two cats, three hamsters, and a rabbit that already shared living space with his family. Jeff lived in a tiny, walk-up apartment. That left me.

"There isn't anyone else who can do it," Grant said reasonably. "We've all agreed that having a dog would be a good thing. You like dogs, and you've got a house with a fenced-in yard, so what's the problem?"

"I live alone! I like living alone."

Grant shook his head. "Not good. It's a bad sign, you know, when someone your age lives like a recluse. We don't want you overcompensating later, and turning into one of those weird little old ladies with a thousand cats. One dog now will stem that tide."

I glowered.

"Seriously, Charlie, he'll be protection for you. You've opened up a big can of worms with this Windrush thing. It's going to put the kibosh on a couple of would-be millionaires."

"They're greedy, not dangerous."

"No point taking chances." Grant patted my hand in avuncular fashion. "Right, then, that's settled. We're getting a dog, and Charlie is going to be its master."

I complained to Carole about it at dinner. Paul and Neil were off at a soccer team banquet, so we'd agreed to meet at Michele's, a tearoom serving light suppers that left plenty of room for dessert. As Carole put it, Michele's blueberry pie was 'to die for.' Predictably, she found the idea of dog hair all over my house hilarious.

"You'll just have to try and find a beige dog, Charlie, so it'll go with all your beige furniture," she said gleefully, shaking out a flowered pink napkin that matched the flowered pink placemats and the flowered pink wallpaper. A little bouquet of pink flowers graced the centre of the table.

I whined, "What do I know about training a dog?"

Carole said blandly, "Maybe you could take lessons from Kevin Shakespeare. I understand he's very good— with dogs, I mean." She held it for a count of three, then collapsed in another fit of laughter.

"I fail to see . . ." I said, with as much dignity as I could muster.

"Well, Neil certainly didn't," Carole said, dabbing at her eyes with her napkin. "He came home demanding to know who 'that man' was, who was making himself at home in your living room. He said you had a very funny look on your face."

"Ha, ha."

"Oh, come on, Charlie, I'm only teasing. Why don't you bring your Kevin over for Thanksgiving dinner with you? I'd like to meet him."

"He lives in Dorset," I said crossly, "and he's not my Kevin."

Sleep eluded me. I told myself it was the three cups of coffee I had drunk with the blueberry pie, not Carole's banter, but I had to admit it bothered me that my house had seemed empty and too quiet after Kevin and Logan left. Punching the pillow into a mushroom under my cheek, I resolutely turned my mind to other things. I went over my lines for the play. I made a mental list of sundries I needed for the house—a new washer for the tap in the bathroom had to be a priority, before the washcloth developed damp mould. Insidiously, thoughts of Kevin Shakespeare kept creeping in.

At five o'clock, I did the only thing possible in the circumstances. I showered, loaded up my knapsack, made a thermos of coffee, and left a message on my machine telling anyone who cared to know that I was heading out to Trail Lake to do some fishing. I never set out into the wilds without letting someone know where I'm going. If I don't make it back for any reason, at least they know where to start looking. On my way out of town I stopped at Donut Delight, open twenty-four hours for your convenience, for a couple of cranberry muffins.

Trail Lake is about two and a half hours due west of Geddes Lake over secondary roads that live up to their name and make four-wheel drive a necessity. Its attraction can be measured in direct proportion to the inconvenience of getting there. On most maps it's just a blue dot among larger blue dots, some of which have names and many of which do not. It lies quietly protected by pine and spruce wilderness, its water clear and clean, still safe from civilization. I planned to spend the day out in the canoe, fishing rod between my knees, trolling the deep weed beds for pickerel. It's the best way I know of emptying my mind, letting it slide into neutral so that new ideas can drift in unimpeded.

By the time I got to the south shore of Trail Lake the muffins were gone and the coffee nearly so. The sun was coming up as I unloaded the canoe from the top of my car and eased it into the water. Early morning mist hung motionless, like a big cobweb, just above the surface of the water. 'Ghost's breath' we called it when we were kids. I tilted my head and watched my own breath streaming airily out to meet it.

For a while I paddled aimlessly, using a stroke my father taught me that begins at the waist and ends with a thrust from the shoulders. I can paddle all day like that without getting tired. It was from my father, too, that I learned my love of the outdoors. Jane never liked getting dirty, but as a child I loved coming home sunburnt and smelly from a day on the lake. It was only in my teens that I began to reject, as a matter of course, what my parent embraced so wholeheartedly. At fifteen it wasn't cool to hang out and go fishing with your dad, much better to lounge around the community pool trying to attract the attention of the six-foot lifeguard. I know it's pointless to say "if only" but I wish my father had lived to see me grow out of that phase. My sense of him is very strong whenever I'm alone on the water.

As I glided along, the mist drifted away and the sun cleared the tops of the trees, chasing dark shadows across the water and into the woods. I headed north, aiming for the spot where a stream hustles importantly into the lake across from a small rocky island. The island boasts a handful of half-hearted pines and scrubby bushes, and is the perfect spot to light a fire and barbecue a fish.

By the time the sun was directly overhead I had caught two nice-sized pickerel. I made a quick trip from island to mainland to collect some stuff for kindling and a pile of dry twigs to burn. It was as I was paddling back to the island that I heard the sound of a small engine plane coming in from the east. Glancing up to spot it, I noticed the clouds were on the move, streaming gracefully out into thin curving lines. I frowned. Mare's tails usually mean a rainstorm coming. This one was maybe half a day off. I'd have to keep my eyes open. There are a lot of places I would rather be during a downpour than out on an open lake. I'd better make sure I had plenty of time to get to one of them.

A float plane buzzed by with the insistent drone of a trapped bee. As it passed over my head it dropped low, skimming the treetops. Though I shaded my eyes against the glare of the sun, I couldn't make out the plane's call letters. I waved anyway, thinking it might be Warren

Cunningham bringing in a party of fishermen or hunters. A few minutes later I heard the engine sound change, then die altogether. Whoever it was had landed on Pigeon Lake, about a mile from where I was. Trail Lake is too narrow to land a plane on, which is another reason I like it so much. Pigeon is a good fishing hole, though. I have hiked in myself more than once, leaving my canoe on the north shore at Trail. It's a fairly easy trip. There's been enough traffic over the years to mark a clear path through the woods.

I dug a match out of a waterproof holder and lit the fire. It caught right away and I grinned, feeling that tremendous sense of accomplishment I always feel whenever I manage to get a camp fire going first try. While the fire heated up, I cleaned and gutted the fish, unearthing some foil from my knapsack to wrap them in. There are few meals as satisfying as those cooked simply over an open fire and I enjoyed every mouthful of that one. When the last scrap was gone, I consulted the sky again. Clouds were building steadily in the west, dimming the sunlight. It was time to move on.

I uncrossed my legs and pushed up against the rock I had been sitting on, heaving myself to my feet. Something hit my right thigh with all the force of a pile driver, slamming me back onto the ground. As I went down, I registered the echo of a rifle shot. I rolled slightly as I fell, scraping my hands and face, feeling the sharp prickle of gorse grabbing at my hair, landing shocked and winded, spread eagled in a dip of rock and at least partially concealed by scrub.

A second shot ricocheted off the rock beside my head,

a small puff of granite exploding inches from my face. A third bullet whined by harmlessly. A fourth thunked into the skinny base of the pine behind me.

I was not an easy target lying flat as I was and partly hidden, and the rapidly fading light made a long shot practically impossible. Which meant the shooter must be on the little neck of rock that crossed the stream at the edge of the lake; it was the only spot close enough. I prayed he didn't have a boat.

All my effort was concentrated on keeping still, on stifling the impulse to shout, "What the hell do you think you're shooting at?" It was clear the guy with the rifle knew exactly what he was shooting at. My only hope lay in letting him believe he had succeeded in his aim.

So far, shock had mercifully numbed my leg, but I knew that pain lurked not far off, in screaming intensity. I could feel the wetness of my blood soaking through my pant leg into the ground below and I wondered almost idly if anything major had been hit, if I would lie there quietly bleeding to death while some murderous bastard with a rifle watched from the shore. Of one thing I was certain: if I stood up, he would pick me off sure as shooting.

Hysteria bubbled in my throat. My God, what an ass I was, playing with words while someone stalked me with a rifle. I lay unmoving through uncountable eons and thought unprintable thoughts.

What a fool I'd been to come all the way out here alone and unarmed, leaving a message on my answering machine telling the shooter where to find me, and how lucky that I'd opted for lunch on the island rather than the mainland. Had he hoped to make my death look like a hunting accident, or had he not thought much at all? Whose face was behind the gun? Was it Larry's? Or had Grant been right in his warning? Had closing down the dump at the Windrush really unleashed homicidal rage in someone? Was it Beare out there, or Donnelly, or even the Dragon Lady, come to slay the enemy for her knight in shining armour? I wanted to know. I would know, I told myself; I would get to him, or her, assuming he didn't get me first, which at the moment seemed more likely.

Nerve-shattering pain kicked in, sending stark messages of disaster and death to my brain. I must have passed out, for when I became aware of my surroundings again, the sky was heavily grey and a light rain had started to fall. A noise registered fuzzily at the edge of my consciousness, but it took me a minute to recognize it as the sound of a plane engine receding to the east and another minute to connect the dots to the float that had landed on Pigeon Lake. The shooter must have hiked over to find me and gone away again thinking he'd left me dead. I wondered why he hadn't waited to make sure.

Then I noticed just how dark it was. The weather must have decided him to hurry on his way. If a lake is bad news in a storm, a small plane is no place to be either. Time, I imagined, would be important to the shooter. He would need an alibi.

My hand went to my thigh, fingering my pant leg, searching out the extent of the damage. I found an entry wound high on the outside but no exit, which meant the bullet was lodged somewhere in my leg. The fact that I was still alive proved no major artery had been hit. Nonetheless, I was bleeding heavily enough to require attention and I woozily set about administering my own first aid.

My knapsack lay where I had left it beside the now defunct campfire. Thin spirals of smoke fought a losing battle with the increasingly aggressive rain, and as I reached for my pack, I mentally thanked God for whoever invented waterproof material.

I always carry basic first aid equipment with me, though this runs more to material for treating sprains and cuts than gunshots. However, I did have some heavy gauze pads in there and after some awkward and painful fumbling around, I managed to clamp them to my leg with my belt. Throughout the proceedings, I cursed steadily at the top of my lungs, an exercise with a therapeutic effect not sufficiently appreciated in medical circles. I groped in the knapsack again, hoping to find something worthwhile in the way of painkillers, but only came up with a couple of aspirins in one of those foil travel packets. Better save them, in case things get really bad I thought. At least I would be able to offer myself the illusion of medicinal comfort.

My next lookout had to be shelter from the rain. The weather was not likely to improve in the foreseeable future and, despite the wonder fabric of my jacket, I was already shiveringly damp. While my island offered little natural protection, I did have the canoe. Force of habit had prompted me to drag it up under the spindly pines when I stopped for lunch. It wasn't difficult, even one-legged, to flip it on its side and prop it up against a tree trunk. That would make for rather cramped quarters, but at least I'd be relatively dry. I squeezed under my aluminium roof while visions of a roaring fireplace and a snifter of warm brandy danced in my head. It was a good thing I'd already eaten. All I had left was a bar of chocolate and the leftover thermos of coffee. They would make a gourmet breakfast for the morning.

While rain popcorned off the canoe, I dozed fitfully and woke at regular, pain-filled intervals for hours until, finally despairing, I tore open the package of aspirins. The pills were over-the-counter medication designed to treat headaches and minor pain, not gunshot wounds. Swallowing them dry made me gag, but the placebo effect was marvellous, which on the one hand was a blessing, but on the other, raised a few unflattering questions about my gullibility. Even the suggestion of relief dulled the throbbing in my leg enough for me to drift off to sleep, thinking as I had the night before, of Kevin Shakespeare. Last night, those thoughts had been irritating; tonight, they were a comfort.

CHAPTER **TWENTY-NINE**

I woke at dawn, shivering and stiff. Gooseflesh pimpled my arms and my teeth chattered, but my right leg was on fire. I half expected it to crumble to ash when I crawled out from under the canoe. Amazingly it did not, but the pain and puffiness told me I had big trouble, and when I tried to stand, the leg gave out. I collapsed weakly back onto the rock, where I concentrated fiercely on controlling intermittent shivers as I took stock of my condition.

A variety of raw patches on my face and hands stung. My teeth were wearing somebody's used socks. It was still drizzling. Good morning, fellow campers.

I cupped my hands, scooping up some lake water to rinse the worst of the grunge out of my mouth. Deprived of caffeine for more than twelve hours, my body felt sluggish, my brain unresponsive. The thermos was cold of course, but I drank the remaining coffee anyway and munched on the bar of chocolate, hoping that the double shot of stimulants would give me the boost I needed to get going. I had to keep my mind off my leg. I was going to have to stand on it, however briefly, in order to flip the canoe back into the water. If I allowed myself to think about the pain, I'd never be able to do it. Once in the canoe, I could sit keeping my weight off the injured leg. I had to look ahead to that moment. If I let the pain encroach, I was finished.

As soon as I tried to stand, pain sent shockwaves of

nausea washing over me. I could feel myself fading. It took more effort of will than I had thought I had in me to bring my little world back into focus. Balancing as much of my weight as I could on my left leg, I managed to heave the canoe over into the water. My body followed of its own accord, propelled by my weight and the force of the shove that had launched the canoe. I landed in the boat with a resounding thud. For a time I simply lay there in a heap, not moving, scarcely breathing, willing the pain away. Eventually I managed to pull myself upright to perch on the stern seat. There was no question of kneeling or even of bending my right leg. I arranged my body so that I could paddle, if not with maximum efficiency, at least with tolerable discomfort.

The day was endless. The rain was endless. The throbbing in my leg was endless.

I paddled and drifted, trying to keep myself on a straight course and failing as dizziness overwhelmed me. My arms moved mechanically, dip, pull, dip, pull, sometimes completing a full stroke, sometimes merely glancing off the surface of the water. Judging by the intensity of the light, I determined it must be midday, maybe early afternoon. The rain had moved slowly off to the east. Pale sunlight glimmered through the trees, offering faint comfort and little warmth. It was a struggle now to keep my head up. Eyelids weighted by pain and fatigue, I found it hard to focus on the approaching shoreline.

The haze in my brain lifted fractionally. Against all odds, I had reached the south shore of the lake; instinct must have kept me going in the right direction. From where I sat drifting in my canoe, I could even see my car, parked where I had left it by a stand of jack pine, shining in the sun like a beacon to welcome me home.

The sudden barking of a dog roused me from my stupor. I heard the short, excited yelps of a hunter sighting its prey. The sound startled me into panic.

Matt Donnelly, I thought despairingly; it was Matt Donnelly with one of his killer animals, come to finish me off even as I neared the shore.

Oh God, I was so close. If only I could reach the car, I could phone for help. My gun was in the glove box. I could shoot the bastard.

I couldn't even land the canoe.

It bumped against the pebbled shore, rocking gently in the shallow water. I had only to rise and step out of it. But my arms shook uncontrollably. Fire burned along my leg and grey mist swirled in my head.

The dog barked again from very close by. I imagined it waiting to spring from the bushes that clustered the shoreline to my left. Feebly, I raised the paddle out of the water and turned toward the sound in a desperate effort to ward off attack. In turning, I bumped my injured leg against the gunwale. An agonizing wash of pain engulfed me and the world faded to black.

CHAPTER **THIRTY**

I surfaced slowly to semi-consciousness, and an argument.

"You can't put flowers in here, Mom, that's so feeb. Charlie doesn't want flowers in her room. You gotta get something else."

"Such as?"

"I dunno. Somethin' to eat, maybe. Or a book or something for her library. Something she'd like."

"There's nothing 'feeb' about flowers, honey. And as soon as Charlie wakes up, we'll ask her what else she wants."

"How long's she going to sleep for, anyway? It's been two days, already."

Two days. Sweet Jesus. The anxiety I heard in Neil Ewing's voice verged on the tearful. He would be trying not to cry, not to give in to the despair he must be feeling at seeing me like this when, not so long ago, he had watched his little sister slip away forever in just such a sleep as this. I struggled to speak, to reassure him, let him know I was, finally, awake; but even as my mouth opened to form the words I could feel myself falling back into the void.

When I woke again, it was evening and the room was empty. A basket of bronze and yellow chrysanthemums blazed on the table beside my bed, looking anything but feeb. On my wrist, a plastic bracelet, property of the

Geddes Lake Cottage Hospital, told me my name and health insurance number. They had the name right. I took the number on trust.

A perky little nurse, looking far too young for the job, padded in on institutional crepe soles. She reminded me, obscurely, of Carole. She was so pleased to see me awake that I half expected a shower of balloons. Instead she dimpled and said, "Well, isn't this great! You've just won me thirty-five dollars in the hospital pool."

"The hospital pool?" I repeated, in a voice as thick as my head.

She nodded brightly. "Just like for hockey games. You know, goals scored at what time in what period. For you, it was what time on what day you'd wake up."

"Not whether?"

"Oh, no. There was never any question of whether. Only when. So, I win."

She was obviously waiting for congratulations, so I offered them. She bobbed her head in acceptance.

"How did I . . ." I began.

The nurse finished for me. ". . . get here? Well, a dog found your body."

She invested the phrase with Alfred Hitchcock overtones. I gaped at her. She giggled.

"Really. These people were out with their dog—two dogs, actually—and the dogs found you, drifting just off shore in a canoe, with a bullet in your leg." She was enjoying the drama. "Naturally, they brought you right in. The dogs had their picture in the paper yesterday. Gorgeous looking things they are, golden retrievers." She grinned at me. "Your picture didn't make it."

The editor of our local newspaper is a long-standing member of the Kennel Club. When he isn't setting type, he breeds and trains hunting dogs. In his paper the doggy angle of any story always gets top billing. From what the nurse had told me, the golden retrievers in this case had to have been Daisy and Donald. They were a far cry from the killers of my fearful imaginings, and I owed each of them the biggest steak bone I could find.

My little nurse plucked the chart off the foot of my bed. "Okay, now, down to business. I'm Nancy—isn't that awful, Nurse Nancy—doesn't it just sound like one of those pre-teen novels? Anything you want, just shout." Giving me no time to voice a request of any kind, Nancy busied herself with a thermometer and a blood pressure cuff. It seemed that nothing vital was missing upstairs after all. Despite the rather inane patter, her professional touch was deft and gentle.

"I'm sure you're dying to know all about yourself," she said, "no pun intended, but I'm only a lowly nurse so you'll have to wait for the voice on high to give you the whole story."

The conspiratorial twinkle in her eye told me what she thought of the doctor's advanced capabilities. I laughed. Nancy made some notations on the chart and hung it back on the foot of my bed. "I'll send Dr. Forbes in right away."

I interpreted "right away" to mean sometime within the next two hours, but, in fact, it was only a couple of minutes before a capable looking older man was staring at me over the rims of his glasses.

"Dan Forbes," he said, shooting out a hand. Through

a hedge of bushy brows, steady grey eyes looked me over carefully; I had the impression they didn't miss much.

"How are you feeling?"

"Disconnected."

I saw the eyebrows go up. "Hardly surprising. You've been out of touch for a couple of days. What about the leg? Any pain?"

"No, not to speak of. I've been trying to decide if that's a good sign or a bad one." I tried hard to keep anxiety out of my voice, but the doctor heard it anyway.

The grey eyes met mine. With gentle deliberation, Dr. Forbes lifted the sheet and blanket from my right leg. He picked up my foot and flexed it so that I could see it, then, slipping a straight pin from his lapel, he jabbed each of my toes in turn. Muscles tensed against bad news relaxed with the sweet sensation of each little pinprick, and at the look of relief on my face when he was finished, the doctor gave a satisfied grunt. "Your leg will be right as rain in a couple of weeks. There was some infection in it when they brought you in, but that's under control now and we got the bullet out. The police are holding on to that."

"The police?"

Dr. Forbes nodded. "It's standard in a shooting incident; they have to be notified." He looked at me curiously, but when I said nothing, he didn't pursue it.

"Why was I unconscious so long?" I asked. "Fever? The infection?"

Forbes gave a short bark of laughter. "Apparently you fell over trying to get out of your canoe. You hit yourself on the head with the paddle." He grinned and I had to laugh. "You were unconscious when your friends hauled you out of the water. Shock, exposure, infection—they all added a little. Your body just decided to shut down for a while, so it could repair some of the damage from within." The doctor glanced at his watch and scribbled something on the chart. "I've got to go. There are plenty of sick people in this place that need my attention more than you do." He gave me a look over the tops of his glasses. "We'll keep you around for local colour for another day or two. If you need anything, just ask Nancy. She's pretty good—if you can stand the chat." He delivered this line with the same dry humour Nancy had shown and I wondered about the connection between them. I found out later she was his daughter.

The medical interlude had just about exhausted me. I wanted nothing more than to sink into the pillows and drift back to sleep, but it wasn't in the game plan. Having surfaced once, I was not going to be allowed to slip away again until I had assisted in some official inquiries.

Constable Bourque interviewed me for the third time, his expression still polite and noncommittal, but much less sceptical.

"The people who brought you in," he consulted a flip pad, "a family by the name of Ewing, had no comment to make beyond the obvious. Their son Neil apparently called your house and got some message about you going fishing out at Trail Lake. When you weren't back by noon the next day, they got worried and went looking. So far, we're officially inclined to view this as a hunting mishap, some hotshot out after ducks pinging you instead and running scared when he realized what he'd done." Bourque eyed me. "Do you have any reason to suspect that the shooting was other than accidental, Ms. Meikle?"

· I had had plenty of time during the endless night and day on the lake to decide how I wanted to answer that one. There was no point in prevaricating. I had already been beaten over the head and shot at more often than was good for me. I'm only a conservation officer, not the Lone Ranger and I decided that now would be as good a time as any to call in the cavalry. Whoever had tried to kill me, the OPP were the ones to figure it out. I told Constable Bourque everything I knew.

By the time I had finished giving my statement, my throat was dry and my head throbbed. The sleep I had longed for an hour ago eluded me now. The knowledge that someone, maybe several someones, wanted me dead was mind numbing. I lay in the semi-dark of my hospital room feeling fragile and abused and very much alone.

CHAPTER **THIRTY-ONE**

Nurse Nancy came bubbling in just as I was finally dozing off. Pale grey light filtered through the gap in the curtains. Pre-dawn, I guessed. It was a hell of a time for someone to want to stick a thermometer in your mouth. Nancy gave me a quick, appraising glance.

"Didn't sleep much, eh?"

"Not much."

"How about a cup of tea? We have some nice herbal stuff at the station that might be just the ticket."

"Sounds good. Let me see if I can totter across to the john first."

Nancy took my elbow and helped me up. I was appalled at how weak and dizzy I felt.

"Not to worry," Nancy said cheerfully, propelling me over to the bathroom door. "It'll pass," she added, giggling at her own pun.

By the time I emerged, I was feeling steadier on my feet and completed an uneventful trip back to bed. The sheets had been straightened, the pillows freshly plumped up. A mug of tea steamed on the bedside table. Nancy had deliberately left the lights dim and I blessed her sympathetic nature as I resettled myself. Ten minutes later I was sound asleep.

The usual hospital sounds made no impression on my slumber, but a voice verging dangerously close to a whine brought me up out of a deep sleep.

"Aw, rats," the voice said. "She's still sleeping. I thought they said she'd finally woken up."

"She has," I said, opening my eyes.

"Charlie!" Neil cried, rushing over to my side. His eyes were bright with the tears that men of eleven are too proud to shed. I gave him a high five. "How's it going, chief?"

Carole gently elbowed her son out of the way and leaned over to give me a hug and a sheaf of newspapers. "Reading material," she said, "for your convalescence, may it be short and sweet." She gave way to Paul, who grabbed my hand in both of his. "Glad to see you back, friend."

"I owe you one."

Paul shook his head. "I'll put it on the tab."

Nancy flitted into the room carrying a tray. "The party started without me, eh? Well, I brought the eats."

Neil made a face as he looked at the tray. It was standard institutional fare. An amorphous grey mass pretending to be meat was accompanied by pale, limp vegetables and a blob of red jello. The soup, however, both looked and smelled unusually good.

"It's homemade," Nancy admitted. "Jan Somers brought it in this morning and made me promise to put it on your lunch tray. I gather it has some secret ingredient in it. Miss Somers wouldn't tell me what it was," she added austerely, "but I can guess. I don't know what the doctor would say."

I laughed, remembering the discussion I had had with Jan about the ordeal bean, and wishing that in this case guilt could be determined by the simple expedient of legume.

Paul dug a couple of loonies out of his pocket and told Neil to wander on down to the gift shop in the lobby to pick up a few supplies. With my blessing, Carole removed the jello from my tray and sat by the window, happily spooning jiggling red blobs into her mouth.

"It's a revolt against good taste," Paul said. "She hates caviar, but goes crazy over jello. Who can figure?"

He perched awkwardly on the remaining visitor's chair. Its functional design didn't encourage long bedside chats.

"I heard something about jello on the radio just the other day," Carole said. "It was on that noon hour talk show, you know the one with Dave Fredericks? The topic was 'entertaining on a budget' and people were calling in with their favourite recipes. Anyway, the guest on the show—I can't think of her name at the moment— she runs a catering service—was talking about fashions in food and how some things that were tremendously popular party foods ten or fifteen years ago just aren't served anymore. And one of the things she mentioned was the good old jellied salad."

"I remember those. Shaved carrots in lime green jello," Paul said.

I nodded. "Or fruit cup in a mould if you wanted to be really fancy."

"Snicker if you must," Carole said, "but there were more than a couple of old dears who phoned in to staunchly defend the jello salad. Not for them arugula and pine nut delight." She rose and put the empty bowl back on my tray. "I like phone-ins; I listen to Dave Fredericks just about every lunch hour. I really missed it when the CBC substituted those pre-taped interviews during their move."

Neil came back from the gift shop carrying the essentials—two bags of chips and a can of pop.

"No cholesterol," he grinned, triumphantly waving a bag in his father's face. "These chips are practically health food."

Paul sighed.

CHAPTER **THIRTY-TWO**

As soon as my visitors had gone, I picked up the newspapers Carole had brought and skimmed over international stories of war, famine, and economic hardship, and national ones of violence, politicking, and economic hardship. Exposé journalism currently specialized in tales of sexual abuse; the church was suffering badly again today. I picked up the local rag last and laughed out loud as it unfolded to a front page picture of Daisy and Donald, straining to look dignified for the camera. I read the story of my rescue, noted that they'd spelled my name wrong, and flipped to the inside spread on the "Pandora's Box of Sludge" being cleared out of the Windrush Mine. Never mind that it was barrels, not boxes, and liquid waste not solid, the accompanying letters to the editor ranged from outrage over the despoiling of our pristine wilderness to demands for compensation from the government for the depletion of fish stocks and loss of potential recreational revenue. That one was written by someone at the Chamber of Commerce. Notably absent was any weighty message from the Save Our Planet organization. Their chief spokesman Frank Dennison had been unavailable for comment.

I thought back to the radio interview in which he had so zealously promoted the idea of using abandoned mine sites as garbage dumps. No wonder. He had already been raking in a small fortune doing just that. The news that he had been doing so illegally would have been bad enough. But unsafely? And for personal gain? As an environmental guru, the guy was finished. Save Our Planet was finished. With the criminal charges and fines that would be levied against them, Dennison, Burden Transport, and all the rest would never do business again. Ruefully, I noted that Paul and I were prominently named as whistle-blowers.

The bedside phone trilled. I'd have to get shot more often; I hadn't felt this popular in years.

"Charlie, it's Bob Morrison. How's the 007 of the conservation world? Are you trying to make the rest of us look dull or what?"

"Eat your heart out, Bob. I just like getting my name in the paper."

"Yeah, it was a nice picture too. It really did you justice, floppy ears and all. Who's the boyfriend?"

"Ha. Ha."

"Paul says you're on the mend."

"You know how it is, Bob: a vodka martini, shaken, not stirred and I'm right back out there hassling the bad guys."

"Now it's my turn to laugh. I'm glad you're okay, though, Charlie. And here's something that should make you feel even better. We got the poacher."

"Really? Who?"

"Larry Taylor. You sure had that one pegged right. And that knife sheath Shakespeare's dog nosed out is the icing on the cake. Taylor's fingerprints are all over it."

"Did he turn himself in or did the police track him down?"

"Neither. His mother dragged him in. I mean that literally. What a performance! Have you ever seen any of those old movies, *Spanky and Our Gang* and stuff like that, where the headmaster at the school gets one of the little brats in a sort of headlock, screwing the kid's ear around and pulling him along like it's a handle? That's the kind of hold Dorrie had on her son. Larry was bent almost double, she's so much shorter than he is. I've no idea how she got his ear in the first place; she'd have needed a stool or something to reach him."

I loved it. The tartar in Dorrie had finally been unleashed and Larry's bluster had proved to be no match for it.

"I thought Larry had left town," I said.

"I guess the little weasel ran out of money. He came sneaking back to cadge some off his mom and she caught him at it."

"When?"

"What?"

"When did she catch him? When did she turn him in?"

"Oh. It was a couple of days ago now, right about the time you were having your little adventure out at Trail Lake. Joan tried to reach you but only got your machine. She left a message, but when you didn't call her back, she got hold of Paul Ewing and the posse took over from there. Some people will do anything for a headline. You booted the poaching story right off the front page."

I put down the phone with a sigh, feeling a bit like a game show contestant who has used one of her lifelines to no good advantage. Bob's news supported the conclusion I'd reached during the restless hours of the night before: from a logistical viewpoint, Larry Taylor was the least likely suspect in my shooting. True, he had made threats, and true, his violent track record spoke against him, but I was pretty sure he couldn't afford to charter a plane and he certainly wasn't a pilot. Frank Dennison, however, was. I knew that from my visit to the SOP offices. So, he might have flown the plane that landed at Pigeon Lake. Which didn't necessarily make him the shooter. After all, he had at least two partners in crime: Donnelly and the Dragon Lady. I thought about that. Dennison, Donnelly, and the Dragon Lady. They sounded like a pop group. "Ladies and gentlemen, here on stage tonight, we are proud to present The Ditchwater Gang, whose smash hit *Toxic Soup* has just been released on the Dead Lake label." The question was why would any of them bother to kill me now? As far as their illegal dumping business went, the shit had hit the fan days before I set out to go fishing. Getting rid of me wouldn't stop the investigation at the Windrush.

I examined it from every angle I could think of and I always came back to the same idea: the attack on me wasn't linked to the mine, but to murder. Whoever had killed Jim Griffith had tried to kill me. Why? Because they thought I knew something that would implicate them in his death. The problem was, I didn't know what it was they thought I knew.

My head hurt. I longed for a good shot of Irene Creighton's brandy. In lieu of that mind-numbing draught, I flipped on the mini TV that Neil had insisted I rent for the duration of my hospital stay.

"Jeez, Charlie, you can't just lie there in bed all day doing nothing!" he'd said. For his parents's benefit he'd added, "There's a lot of fine educational programming on during the day," but he'd given me an exaggerated wink that suggested my time would be better spent watching the cartoons and sitcoms we were both addicted to.

A burst of applause told me that one of these was about to begin. A voice advised me that the show had been taped before a live studio audience. I felt a cartoon light bulb go on over my head and I sat up with a jolt that sent a shockwave down my leg. Taped, he'd said, the show was taped for later broadcast. Carole had mentioned something about taping too and how much she'd missed the live CBC phone-ins during the studio's move. I scrabbled through the newspapers, looking for the *Globe*. I'd only glanced over it earlier, more interested in the local news than the national, but a story in the business section had caught my eye. Yes, there it was. "New Home for CBC." On the facing page was a critical commentary about the wisdom of such an investment in this time of fiscal hardship.

Live broadcasts had been replaced by pre-taped shows for the dates in question. One of them was the date I was looking for, the day I had listened to Frank Dennison being interviewed by Dave Fredericks. If Dennison had not been in the CBC studio that Monday afternoon, maybe he had been at Finger Lake. And maybe he'd made a return trip for a shot at me. It would have been easy enough for him. He didn't even need to charter a plane; he had his own, which made a wilderness hit-and-run very possible.

Maybe he was more closely related to Don Corleone than I'd thought.

CHAPTER **THIRTY-THREE**

Somewhere between "eureka" and "I hope they nail him to the wall" I fell asleep, not with a gentle drift down a gradual incline, but with a sharp plummet off a steep cliff into blackness. I slept heavily for a long time and woke refreshed and ravenously hungry shortly before noon the next day. There was marked improvement in my leg; it supported me easily, if not painlessly, all the way to the john and back.

"What happened to hospital policy?" I demanded when Nancy came in a few minutes later with my lunch tray. "I thought you guys were dedicated to the concept of waking people up to give them pills to help them sleep."

She gave me a wan smile. "Sorry, we didn't have time for that last night. Emergency was stacked to the rafters." She leaned wearily against the end of my bed. "There was an accident out on the highway just outside town. A bunch of kids coming back from a party over in Rushton were run off the road. The driver is dead." Nancy drew a shaky breath. "The passenger in the front seat—a beautiful girl, God you should have seen her—will never walk again. We med-evaced her out to Toronto this morning. The three others are less of a mess, but only just."

"My God," I said, "what happened?"

"That creep Larry Taylor," Nancy said bitterly. "He was drunk, of course, going like smoke and weaving all over the place. The guy behind him said the kids never had a chance." Her eyes were bright with tears. "The only good thing is, Taylor was killed too. He ran head on into a tree, which was only poetic justice if you ask me."

"Larry Taylor?"

"Yeah, the scourge of Geddes Lake."

"But I thought his truck had been impounded. He's facing charges, for God's sake."

"Tell it to Grampa."

"Les?"

"That's right. Larry's truck was taken away from him, so Grampa lent him his car." She blinked hard, trying to clear the tears. "Too bad he wasn't in it too."

I thought of all the broken lives and heartache that Larry had left behind him. One way or another this tragedy would touch just about every family in town. I thought of Larry's mother, who had finally taken a stand against her hulking, destructive son. Poor Dorrie, where would she find the strength to carry the new burden he had dropped on her? But mostly, I thought about the mischance that had allowed so many innocent people to be in the wrong place at the wrong time. Nausea twisted my stomach. Guilt, like a symptom of illness, suffused my body when I considered my own part in what had happened. If I hadn't pushed so hard, if I hadn't stuck my nose into family business that was patently not my own, would last night have ended differently? I told myself that Larry Taylor had always been a disaster waiting to happen to someone and that if it hadn't been the kids last night it would have been someone else another night. There wasn't much consolation in the thought.

My appetite had vanished. Only the coffee held any

appeal at all. It was weak and lukewarm, but I drank it anyway and as I moved to put my coffee cup back on the tray, I dislodged a piece of paper that had been balancing on the edge of the table. I unfolded it and read: "Dear Charlie, You said I could use your computer for my school project. I was hoping you'd be awake by now, but Dad said you probably wouldn't mind if I just used your machine anyway. He gave me his key. He wants you to call me at your place when you do wake up." Neil had signed his name with a flourish I could only hope he would outgrow. Smiling, I reached for the phone.

Three rings, a click, and I heard my own voice telling me I was heading out to Trail Lake to do some fishing. I'd have to ask Neil to update that message for me while he was there. The machine beeped. I said, "Neil, it's Charlie. Since you haven't answered the phone, I assume you're either in the can or at the fridge. Call me back at . . ." I recited the number printed on the receiver. While I waited for Neil to return my call, I sorted through the newspapers littering my bedside. I wanted to save the one featuring Daisy and Donald. It would look good in my scrapbook.

Ten minutes passed with no word from Neil. What was the kid doing that he couldn't hear the phone? If he had my stereo cranked up to max again, I'd kill him. Last time he'd forgotten to turn it down before he left. When I flipped it on at suppertime, it just about shattered my eardrums. I redialled, and after four rings the machine picked up again. Odd. I reread Neil's note. The scrawl at the bottom said eleven AM It was only twelve thirty now. I doubted he had gone from the hospital to my place, booted up the computer and done all the work on his project in an hour and a half. Especially when the hour and a half stretched over lunchtime. Maybe he'd gone outside. If he'd brought Daisy and Donald with him, which was likely, he might have given them the run of the yard and he'd be out cleaning up after them. I'd threatened a lifetime ban on dogs after I'd wandered out in bare feet one summer morning and skidded through the muck they'd left the night before. Since then, Neil had been meticulous with his scooper. I waited a few minutes and tried my number again. This time, even voice mail didn't pick up.

I felt a tremor of apprehension. Neil wouldn't unplug my answering machine. Neither would his parents, who were the only people Neil would let in when I wasn't there. Was there someone else in the house with him? Someone, perhaps, who hoped to lay a trap for me? The timing was right for it. With all the cutbacks to health care, the hospital was chronically short of beds; anyone who read the paper could know my injury wasn't life-threatening and that I'd be out in another day or two. All they had to do was wait. If Neil got in the way. . . .

I started to call 911, but hung up again before I got to the final 1. Fear prickled my scalp. If I was right, there was a murderer in my house—someone who had been successful once, and who had been willing to try it again. I'd heard it got easier each time, a theory I didn't want to test. A wailing siren or flashing light could panic the killer, and Neil could be dead before the police reached the door. I stamped down hard on the thought that he might be dead even now.

The jeans I had set out to go fishing in were history, but Carole, bless her, had brought me some sweats and runners. I threw them on and left. No one tried to stop me. The hospital staff was still busy trying to pick up the pieces of last night's disaster. Little knots of people huddled together in the lounge, their faces strained with grief. A grey-haired nurse moved among them, offering coffee and comfort foods in lieu of hope. My stomach clenched at the haunting tragedy in the parents's eyes. I had seen it before, when the doctor told Paul and Carole their daughter was gone. I thought of what the loss of their son would do to my friends, and I felt the explosive fury that had so recently erupted in the Taylor kitchen flare then freeze into implacable purpose.

I stole a bicycle from the rack in front of the hospital praying its owner wouldn't mind too much when he found out why I'd taken it. My house was only half a mile away, and luckily for my leg, all downhill. The road was deserted, the town silent, already shrouded in mourning.

I ditched the bike under a bristly spruce with the fleeting hope that it would be safe there until I could retrieve it, then made my way round through the woods that edged my property. My right leg burned, my left vibrated with the strain of bearing all my weight. Peering out from behind a screen of branches, I could see that my living room shades were drawn. That was to be expected; at this hour of the day, the light that poured in through the picture window reflected blindingly off the computer screen. Neil would have adjusted the shades as a matter of course. As I edged around to the side of the house, I could see his bike propped up against a tree. There was nothing to indicate anyone else was in the house, but only a fool would have driven right up to the door when there were plenty of bushes to hide a car in just up the road. My own vehicle was parked in its usual spot under a sheltering pine. Paul and Carole had brought it back from Trail Lake after getting me to the hospital. Unless someone had removed it for some unknown reason, my gun should still be locked in the glove box.

I made a brief detour into the tool shed, where I keep a spare key hidden in a flowerpot. Clutching it tightly in my hand, I covered the short distance to the car at a crouching, limping run, sickly aware of how visible I'd be to anyone looking out the kitchen window. Bob Morrison's crack about 007 had seemed funny at the time, but the coldness that had settled on me at the hospital had not thawed, and I could no longer see the humour in, or weigh the foolishness of, my actions.

I crept up to my own back door like a thief. Cautiously, I tried the knob, and was relieved to feel it turn under my hand. I said a silent prayer of thanks for oiled hinges.

There was no one in the hall when I eased through the door, and I stood there for a long moment, tensed and listening. From the living room came the faint hum of the computer monitor, punctuated by a low, intermittent rumble that sounded uncannily like the growling of a dog. I felt the hairs rise on the back of my neck. This was an element I hadn't bargained for. Images of the mutilated body of Luther flashed through my head. I remembered with dread the size and strength of the dogs patrolling the yard at Burden Transport. If one of those dogs had been sicked on Neil. . . . My fingers tightened convulsively on the gun in my hand, the cold weight of it reassuring. I forced myself to breathe deeply, evenly, ears straining all the while for any indication that the dog had noted my presence in the house.

Outside, the crisp stillness of the day was suddenly and rudely shattered by the ululating wail of a police siren that brayed with growing insistence as it approached my house. Who might have called them, I didn't stop to wonder. The only thought in my mind was what might happen to Neil if the intruder in my house panicked. I burst through the doorway into the living room and crouched, knees bent, feet apart, gun levelled and steady, making a slow sweep of the room.

Three pairs of eyes regarded me with shock. Two golden retrievers wagged their tails briefly in my direction, but did not shift from their position by the cupboard door. Beside them, Neil stared up at me in amazement. His lips opened and closed soundlessly a couple of times before he managed to croak, "Charlie?"

I straightened slowly, arms wilting to my sides. From inside the cupboard came the plea, "Get those dogs away from me!" And outside, a voice on a bullhorn ordered me to come out with my hands up; they had the place surrounded.

Forget 007; this was pure *Keystone Cops*.

CHAPTER **THIRTY-FOUR**

Daisy and Donald made the front page again. "Canines Corner Culprit" screamed the banner. The story lavished praise on the animals, acknowledged their young master's courage, and mentioned my name only in passing.

Neil had, in fact, been outside the first time I phoned and he hadn't bothered to check for voice mail when he came back in the house. He was sampling the contents of my fridge when I called again, but by the time he realized the phone was ringing, Teddy Beare had burst in, looking anything but cuddly. As I'd feared, he'd intended to ambush me when I came home. He didn't realize I'd already twigged to his dual identity and informed the police of it. He still thought killing me might save at least some of his fortunes. His surprise at finding Neil in my kitchen was total.

Seeing the open fridge, and assuming I was the one looting it, Beare had rushed into the room wielding a baseball bat and shouting obscenities over the din of heavy metal booming from the stereo. The dogs were on him in a flash. Normally friendly, they had attacked without hesitation when their boy was threatened. In the mêlée, a lamp was knocked over and a potted fern upended on the carpet. Terrified by the barking dogs, Beare had dropped the bat and turned tail, but Daisy and Donald had blocked his retreat with bared teeth until, in desperation, he had sought refuge in the closet. Neil had gamely commanded the dogs to "watch" while he called the police and, like a good actor settling into his role, Donald had supplied the growls. He willingly reenacted his role for TV journalists, though I gathered the gleam in his eye so faithfully reproduced in the tabloids had less to do with stardom than with impending fatherhood.

"Who unplugged the answering machine?" I asked.

Neil grinned. "That creep tripped over the cord when he was trying to get away from Daisy."

I was relieved to hear that Neil's voice had finally dropped back into its usual register. In answer to my call, Paul and Carole had appeared at my front door only minutes after the police took Beare in hand. Neil had been shaking with reaction and residual fear. His mother had wrapped him in a blanket and installed him on the couch with a protective arm firmly around his shoulders and a new pucker of worry around her eyes. Paul produced hot chocolate laced with brandy. Neil downed it with surprising speed.

"He has the makings," I said.

Carole gave me a small smile and I wondered how long it would be before the old glow returned.

When Neil was able to answer questions, Constable Bourque prodded him gently over the details of what had happened. Neil answered him in a thin, high voice that stumbled in the rush of words. I saw the worry deepen on Carole's face. As the brandy took effect, Neil began to relax a little, and I watched him gradually renegotiate the reality of a frightening situation into something bearable, even heroic.

Once he was in handcuffs, Beare broke down almost

at once, hurrying to implicate the general manager at Burden Transport, but protesting the innocence of the Dragon Lady, whose name, oddly enough, turned out to be Estella, which made me wonder if her mother had attended the same school as mine.

The Toronto police arrested Matt Donnelly in his office in spite of his claim that he knew nothing about what was being transported in his trucks. He defied anyone to prove he had ever been to the Windrush Mine. Beare continued to assert that Jim Griffith's death had been accidental, and since I had survived his attack on me, I had no doubt his lawyer would successfully plead a lesser charge than murder. It all seemed grossly unfair. So much damage done, so little retribution exacted for it.

Laura added what she could to the growing file of evidence against Beare. The charges laid under the *Environmental Protection Act*, at least, would stick.

The mess at Jim's cabin had been cleared up by a pair of guys who looked uncomfortably like Curly and Moe, but who ran a very efficient cleaning company called Orderly. They hauled away the remnants of my old friend's life and scrubbed down the insides of his home. One of them, I'm not sure which, carefully removed the flies that had been studded into Jim's rainbow. I offered them to Laura, but she declined. Joan suggested mounting them in a glass case and hanging them in our office. They'll look good with the painted table.

Laura put the sale of the cabin on hold. As long as the future of Finger Lake was in doubt, there wouldn't be much of a market.

"What will happen to it?" Laura asked, when she called. "The lake, I mean. Will it die? Can the pattern of destruction be reversed once it's begun?"

"I don't know. Given time, maybe. Given time, animal populations can be restored, forests can grow back and, yeah, lakes can even cleanse themselves. Assuming, of course," I added, "that the elements that clobbered them in the first place stand still."

"He hasn't stopped dancing since the vet confirmed Daisy's pregnant." Carole said. There was some animated discussion over what to do with the pups. Neil was all for keeping the entire litter, but even Carole's romantic soul could not encompass a house overrun with puppies, however cute. As purebreds they would be worth a considerable sum, and as the offspring of heroes, even more. I was pretty sure they'd all be spoken for before they'd even been born and I resolved to get my bid in early. I had developed quite an affinity for dogs over the past few weeks. Maybe I'd buy two and make a present of the second one to Irene Creighton.

Over my feeble protests, Carole had called Kevin Shakespeare, told him the whole story, and invited him up for Thanksgiving dinner. When he rang my bell, I had just finished the crust for a pumpkin pie, and I answered the door with floury hands. Tracker that he was, Logan immediately picked up the scent, and stationed himself between the counter and the fridge, just where I would most easily trip over him and perhaps spill something for him to clean up.

"What about the boys?" I asked.

"Still with their mother. By the way," he said, "I

brought you a present." His fingers brushed mine lightly as he handed me a small, wrapped box.

I felt nervous as I tore off the decorative tissue paper; it seemed a little early in our friendship for gifts. Warily, I lifted the lid. Inside the box, nestled in more tissue, lay a washer for the bathroom tap.

Around two we got in the car and headed down the road toward a weathered signpost whose neatly chiselled letters read James Griffith (Fisherman). Logan eyed the pie left cooling on the counter with regret, but he perked up when we turned down the rutted track to the cabin. Kevin wanted to see it now that it had been cleaned up, and I wanted to spend a little time communing with Jim. I wanted to let him know that I'd found what he had to show me that fateful Monday, and to reassure him that somebody was looking after his lake.

My leg was healing well, but the muscles still tired quickly, and on the path down to the lake I leaned heavily on my walking stick. The water looked very blue against the crimson and gold of the bordering forest, the colours blended at the horizon by an Indian summer haze. A vee of geese honked overhead, the last wave in the tide of feathered creatures flowing south for the winter. One maverick in the group came hurtling down in front of me, feet set as if for a landing, but he only skidded across the water, dipping briefly before taking off again, hurrying to rejoin his fellows. The small disturbance he'd created on the surface settled back to mirror calm, leaving no hint of the troubled undercurrent below.

ANNE METIKOSH was born in Montreal, raised in Toronto and has lived in Halifax, Yellowknife and Burlington. She now makes her home in Calgary, Alberta, with her husband, daughter, two dogs and a horse.

The author of numerous articles, and short stories, Metikosh has published a young adult fiction titled *Terra Incognita,* and had her writing featured in the anthologies, *The Little Iron Horse* and *Chicken Soup for the Parent's Soul.* Her part-time job juggling figures gives her time to indulge her true passions: riding horses, reading mysteries, and writing.